BLUE BLOOD WOLF

BIG WOLF ON CAMPUS
BOOK SIX

AIDY AWARD

PIPER FOX

BLUE BLOOD WOLF

She thought finding her very own Prince Charming at Bay State University was nothing more than a fairytale. Then a real-life prince proved her wrong. But her happy ever after comes with more than a crown... he also has claws and fur and howls at the moon.

Stacia's life is one coffee-fueled shift at work or class at a time, all while saving for law school. Her only escape is the royal romances she loves to read. But when a mysterious British transfer student crashes into her world, everything changes. Bash, with his nerdy glasses and swoon-worthy accent, is so much more than just a charming stranger.

Bash only wanted a brief escape from the suffocating duties of royalty, but fate had other plans. Stacia ignites a fire in him he can't ignore. Claiming her should have been impossible, yet his wolf knows she's the one. But secrets have consequences, and Bash's double life is a ticking time bomb.

With a dangerous pack of one-blood wolves threatening

campus and Bash's royal responsibilities calling him home, love might not be enough to keep them together. Stacia and Bash will have to risk everything for a chance at a fairytale happy ever after.

Blue Blood Wolf is a steamy, suspenseful paranormal romance featuring a royal wolf shifter, a curvy heroine who is so much more than a princess, and a fated mates love story that defies tradition.

I was totally going to be late to work today. But the biggest news to hit Bay State University since the announcement that Prince Ruslan Bashkir was coming here on his grand tour of the United States just blew up the entire internet. "Holy crap, you guys. Have you seen the sitch?"

Nobody better to share the gossip with than my book besties at the Moon Bean bookstore. The guys at the Wolves' Den Bar and Grill would totally not care about a missing crown prince. Don't get me wrong, bartenders were huge gossips, but my coworkers didn't give a hoot about the royal family of Bashkiria.

"Hey, Stacia. We got in that royalty romance series you ordered. Wait, what situation?" Selena, the Moon Bean's owner, waved at me from the cash register and then looked around like there was paparazzi behind her or something. Rosie didn't even look up from where she was bent over her laptop at the table in the corner, probably hard at work on her latest romance novel. Something rattled in the back, probably Charlize puttering around.

I held up my phone. "How could you miss it? The internet is exploding. Prince Ruslan is missing."

Selena rolled her eyes but smiled at me. She understood.

Maybe I was a little bit obsessed with the royals. I bought my ticket to the Queen of Bashkiria's talk at the student center approximately point five seconds after they went on sale. I was not missing this chance to get up close and personal with a real life royal. I couldn't stop myself from talking about, thinking about, dreaming about meeting Prince Ruslan Bashkir since their tour of America had been announced. He was the world's most eligible bachelor.

And I was the world's oldest virgin bachelorette. I wasn't kidding myself that he'd want to hook up and whisk me back to his castle in Bashkiria. I wasn't princess material. Not with my muffin top, jiggly thighs, and so very American upbringing and accent.

I simply wanted to see him in person, maybe be swept away with a kiss where I get to push my fingers into his sexy dark curls. Hear him whisper sweet nothings in my ear in his Bashkirian accent. Ooohh. Shivers.

I shoved my phone, open to the BBC's report, in Selena's face. I accidentally bumped the elbow of a guy standing near the cash register with a newspaper up to his face in my hurry to reach Selena or Charlize. His big nerdy glasses and his paper went flying like in a cartoon, scattering everywhere.

"Oops. Sorry about that." I squatted down to help pick up the mess.

He knelt, snagged his glasses, shoving them back on his face, sadly covering his pretty golden eyes that sparkled, and then gathered what I hadn't. "Don't worry about it."

Under his breath I heard him whisper, "Bollocks. I was hoping not to have to pay for that."

Whoo-boy. He had the yummiest European accent ever, all posh and proper… and panty melting. Exchange student maybe? I was an awful flirter, but this was too good of an opportunity. I had to try. Besides, maybe he knew the British royal family.

"From one poor college student to another, let me get that for you." I picked up his paper and set it on the counter along with the stack of books Selena had ready for me. An awkward laugh slipped out with my words, because I was definitely a huge dork and not good at talking to guys. Oh geez, what was I even doing?

He stared at me like I'd grown twenty-two heads. Must not be the custom in Europe or wherever he was from to be friendly like that. Or was it my obnoxious American laugh? I'd heard Europeans all thought we were loud.

But his slightly horrified, definitely surprised look turned into a smile that had me forgetting how to breathe. "Cheers, but not necessary."

He practically bolted out of the bookstore and left me with only Selena there for the emotional support I needed after being bowled over by a severe case of the swoonies.

"You listen to me right now, Stacia." Selena had that you're-in-trouble mom tone going on and it pulled me out of my lusty fantasy.

No, I was not imagining him wearing a crown and nothing else. Shut up. I'm not all hot and bothered, you're hot and bothered. Just because he sort of looked like Prince Bashkir, didn't mean he'd be up for a little prince and princess role play.

"If you don't go hunt that boy down and kiss the European daylights out of him, you're fired." Selena wagged her finger at me.

Snort. Like he'd be interested in me. With an accent like that, every girl on campus would be falling at his feet with her legs wide open. "He clearly wasn't into me and also... I don't work here anymore."

She'd already fired me for how many days I'd taken off. Well, she didn't fire me. She found me a new job at the bar next door. I made more money there because of…honestly, my big boobs got me some great tips. So I didn't have to work as much.

"Uh, yes he was. I'll call Liam over at the Wolves' Den and tell him he has to fire you."

"He's going to fire me anyway if I don't clock in, like, five minutes ago. Put these on my account?" I grabbed the stack of books and bolted for the door.

I'd just reached for the handle when Selena grabbed my arm and hissed, "Wait."

The sound of a bunch of motorcycles tearing down the street cut off any questions I was going to ask. A bunch of male voices called back and forth, and the laughter had a nasty edge to it, definitely at someone, not with. It made me glad I hadn't just stepped out the door.

Selena still had a tight grip on my arm as she watched the last of the bikers go by, and I could have sworn I heard her growl down low in her chest, but it was probably just the echo of the engines.

"Whew, that was close." I flashed Selena a smile. "Thanks."

She blinked like she'd forgotten she was still clutching my arm and finally let go. "Be careful out there. And don't forget what I said."

Right, like I was just going to go stalk and mack on an English hottie. But I didn't say that, just in case she really was going to call Liam and get me fired. She wouldn't, would she? Nah.

As Selena sauntered back toward the Moon Bean's bookshop counter, she shook her head and muttered to herself. "Niko needs to do something about those one-bloods. Showing their faces here like they aren't even scared."

I only understood about half of what she was saying.

There was a motorcycle gang that had been showing up in the area a lot more, even coming right onto the campus, but I had no idea what a one-blood was. Maybe it was a biker term? I couldn't really picture Selena, bossy, matchmaking Selena, using biker lingo though.

The alarm on my phone blared, and I jumped bad enough that I almost dumped my precious books on the ground. Crapballs, I was going to be late if I didn't hustle. Good thing the Wolves' Den was right next door. After one last glance to make sure the coast was clear, I ran across the alley to the bar. It only took a minute to throw my stuff in my locker and clock in, and then it was balls to the wall with serving drinks.

I both loved and hated coin night at the Wolves' Den. Super busy, but the one night that was not the best tips. Except for our resident bad boy bartender, Ty. One smile from him had the wallets of all the women practically being thrown at him.

But I knew a secret the customers didn't. He was taken. My friend Hunter had snagged his heart hard. They were grossly adorable together.

"Stacia, can you work a double tomorrow? I haven't found a new waitress yet." Liam poured me a tray of quarter beers for the table of football players who'd sat down in my section.

"I see Selena hasn't called yet, so yes. No take-backsies." Ha. I'd heard stories from the girls at the Moon Bean about Selena's matchmaking machinations, and I was not getting sucked in. I was going to have to skip out of the last ten minutes of my poli-sci class to get to the shift, but I needed the money. My scholarship for law school next year covered tuition and books but not moving expenses and someplace to live in New Haven.

"Oh, she called." He waggled his eyebrows at me. "Said to tell you you're fired if you don't—"

"Sorry, can't hear you," I shouted and grabbed my tray. Lucky for me we were swamped the rest of the night and Liam didn't bring up my faux firing again.

That night in my dreams, instead of Prince Ruslan, I saw the sparkling golden eyes and brown skin of that English guy from the bookstore. After all the naughty things he did to me in my sleep, I had a hard time getting out of bed for class. I slogged through eighteenth-century European history and my global economics classes. I didn't even have the energy to care about the Ruslan Watch posts in my FaceSpace feed.

I grabbed a cheap coffee at the student center to make it through my dreaded poli-sci class. Stupid pre-law requirements. At least it was one of those big lecture halls with hundreds of students, so if I sat in the back and rested my eyes, the professor wouldn't even notice.

I slid into a seat next to a dude who was clearly doing the same thing as I was. He had the hood of his Bay State University Dire Wolves sweatshirt pulled up and sat slumped down in the seat. Perfect. He wouldn't tattle if I fell asleep.

"Mind if I sit here?" I pulled out my notebook like I was going to take notes, thinking it would make a great pillow, and set it on the fold-up armrest desk, then glanced at my partner in slacking.

Tired golden eyes behind big nerdy glasses looked back at me, blinked a few times, and then the guy gave me a half-smile of recognition. "Are you stalking me, princessa?"

Hashtag melted panties.

BASH

This whole escape from my royal guards so I could go undercover was proper cocked-up. Nothing was working out one wit like I'd thought it would. Being on the lam without use of my phone, credit cards, or social status was harder than I imagined it to be. Neither of my cousins had mentioned any of that when we cooked up this scheme.

Should have known better than to take advice from the two biggest scandals to hit the royal wolf family this century. Who even believed in fated mates anyway? Both bastards had claimed to have found theirs and taken humans as mates.

Ridiculous.

I hadn't even thought to exchange what little bit of cash I had on hand. Good job, Bash. Just hand over some Bashkirian coins, that wasn't going to immediately give me away. I was absolute bollocks at this whole secret identity thing.

I'd slept in a fucking library last night and this morning nicked some poor student's gym bag for a change of clothes and something called a breakfast burrito before sprinting across campus to practice just as the other Dire Wolves were arriving.

It was all completely exhilarating.

Playing Rugby back home had at least given me enough skills to make out like I belonged on the football team, and I had to admit, there was something exhilarating to the sport. I doubted I'd be able to stick around long enough to actually play a game though.

The local wolf shifters hiding in plain sight on the team had agreed to not only be some cover for me, but also help me track the fucking one-bloods. They didn't like those pieces of shit skulking around their town or their mates.

They were all good lads, the lot of them, and those that were slated to be alphas someday like me would make good allies.

I figured I had maybe another twenty-four to forty-eight hours before the Queen's guards tracked me down. That should be more than enough time to hunt down the one-bloods' lair and talk my way into a cute American bird's pants. Like the stunning lass who'd just sat down next to me. The very same girl I'd jostled with at the bookstore.

There was something about her that had my wolf very, very interested. I swear her soft white skin had a glow about it.

Marking her, claiming her, and mating with her was absolutely not what I should be thinking about.

When the Wolf Tzar had reached out to Bashkiria for help in rooting out the one-bloods—werewolf supremacists who thought that we were all superior to humans—who'd been a thorn in his side since he took over and took his own human as his mate, the queen, the royal guard, and I had crossed the pond under the guise of a royal visit.

A lot of the one-blood activity had been centered around the university campus though. I'd ditched my entourage and gone undercover as a transfer student so I had a chance of finding out what the bloody idiots were doing here, or what it was they wanted, with a little bit of blind hope that I might just be able to stalk them back to whoever was in charge of the gang.

And if doing my duty allowed me a few days of freedom and the chance to chat up a gorgeous American girl who smelled like delicious ripe peaches and had my wolf's ears pricking up with interest, well then, that was all the better.

Especially since she was the first woman my wolf side had ever taken an interest in.

I knew I'd pay later for this little bout of freedom, but eyeing the lass's full lower lip and mouthwatering curves, I couldn't exactly bring myself to care.

"Are you stalking me, princessa?" I didn't know why I said that. She had admitted to being a royals fanatic yesterday. I should stay far, far away from her.

But who was I to deny destiny? My birthright was what put me into this situation in the first place. I had no choice in being the crown prince of Bashkiria. But fate? Seemed that even though I didn't believe in it, if that fickle goddess was going to throw this woman in my path again, I could take the hint.

It's not like she'd be my fated mate. That was only a fairy-tale. And only in recently in America did wolves get to chose their own mates. I'd be mated to someone who would boost the family either in reputation or power.

Certainly not a sweet American.

She laughed out loud and then covered her mouth when the row of students in front of us turned to stare. Every emotion this girl had was written across her face and she let them all out, hiding nothing. Including the lust sparkling in her eyes, even if it was tinged with a bit of embarrassment.

How nice it must be to behave in such a way. Her pure

American-ness had my interest piqued. My cock's too. Not to mention my wolf had already thoroughly chosen her as candidate number one for sowing my wild oats with.

She was about to slink down into the seat, and that would be the end of my brief flirtation with her. Nope. That was not happening. I had precious little time and wanted to make the most of it. With her. I grabbed her notebook and her hand and pulled her up and out of her seat. "Come on, let's get out of here."

There were way too many people looking at us anyway. Eventually someone would see through my nerdy glasses disguise.

She squeaked adorably, grabbed her knapsack off the seat, and squeezed my hand. "Are you kidnapping me?"

A stalker and a kidnapper, match made in heaven. "Quite. Come along quietly and I won't have to spank you."

Her eyes went wide at my dirty implication, but she was definitely interested. My kind of girl. We hurried out the back entrance to the hall and into the large courtyard. The early afternoon sunshine was no place to kiss the girl in private, and that was all I wanted to do.

Something about her had my libido on overdrive. Probably the fact that she had no idea who I was and her attraction wasn't influenced by my position. Her magnificent tits didn't hurt either.

That damn smell of ripe peaches had my mouth watering. I couldn't wait to get a proper taste. My wolf pressed close to the surface, enough to have my teeth feeling a bit too sharp in my mouth, and I had to coax it back down. Having a beautiful bird run screaming from me because she caught a glimpse of a mouthful of wolf fangs wasn't on my agenda.

I dragged her along to a circle of benches under a copse of large old trees outside the library. We were all alone, exactly the way I wanted her. The clock was ticking and the sooner I could romance her, the sooner we could get naked. I wondered if students really had sex in the stacks at the library as I'd seen in movies. That sounded like fun to me.

Sex of any sort sounded like fun. There was no way I was waiting until my mating ceremony like my father insisted. One too many half-royal pups running around the castle, thanks to more randy cousins, and he had me and my social life under lock and key.

All I ever did was train, hunt, train some more, and make the occasional appearance where I had to pretend to be a mere human.

This tour of America, undercover or not, and this girl were my one chance to lose my virginity before I was mated. I pulled her down onto my lap. "What's your name, love?"

She squirmed as if uncomfortable sitting on my leg, but I wrapped my arms around her plump rear end and held her tight.

"Anastasia, like the princess, but people call me Stacia. You're from England, right? Or, oh, I guess you could be from some other part of Europe, but I'm pretty good at telling the difference. Geez, you've got me all flustered, I'm rambling and I haven't even asked your name." Her cheeks went pink, and I wanted to cup them between my hands and feel their warmth.

"I'm—" I had it all planned out that I would call myself some working man's name like Harry or George. But I didn't want to lie to her. I wasn't sure my wolf would let me if I tried. Nobody ever saw me for me, and just once I wanted someone to. "I'm Bash."

Thank fuck for my years at Eton and Cambridge for teaching me a British accent I could hide behind. It all added to the exchange student disguise. Ladies all around the world went a little weak in the knees for that James Bond thing. Or so the media led me to believe. I might as well give that a try.

"I'll say whatever you like and be from wherever you want me to be if you'll kiss me."

"What? Me?" Stacia scrambled off my lap and stood up. Her mouth hung open, and she stared at me. She looked around like I was talking to someone else.

I snagged her arms and gave them a tug to pull her between my legs. "Definitely you."

"Oh... oh." She blinked a bunch of times and glanced at me sideways through those long lashes.

Did she genuinely not know how gorgeous she was? How refreshing. The upper-class wolftresses in my social circles knew exactly how good looking they were and how to use that to their advantage. Every move, every scent, used to the best advantage. Not Stacia. Even her nickname was the opposite of the posh toddy's looking to become the next Princess of Bashkiria.

I took her face between my hands and brought her mouth down to mine. Her breath was spicy cinnamon and coffee, and I couldn't wait to taste her. Her lips parted on a soft sigh and her eyes fluttered shut. I brushed my bottom lip across hers and it was like electricity.

Her tongue darted out and my brain shut down, gobsmacked. My cock grew so hard I thought it was going to bust out. I sure as hell wanted it to. I needed her hands wrapped around me, or even better, her luscious mouth. My teeth pricked the inside of my lips, and I had to take a few deep breaths.

My wolf wanted me to bite her, to claim her, and I couldn't. Not just because I was lying to her about who and what I was, or that Stacia wasn't likely to react well to me sinking me teeth into her throat, but also because the future King of Bashkiria would be mated in a public ceremony to a wolftress, one chosen by my parents. That was my duty, what my country demanded.

But this right here, with Stacia warm and sweet and in my arms, smelling of peaches, that could be just for me.

I was about to drag her inside the building and see if I couldn't find one of those dark corners and get her legs wrapped around my waist, but her phone went off with the tune of 'God Save the Queen' and all my plans and my cock went crashing down.

"Sorry. Crap." She grabbed the offending thing out of her jeans pocket and glanced at it. "I gotta go to work. Dammit."

"Can't you skive off?" I would quite happily spend the entire rest of the day and into the night exploring her mouth and every single one of her curves.

Except for the part where I was supposed to be hunting the one-bloods. Only a woman this… perfect could make me forget my duties.

"Skive? Oh, you mean skip work? Like play hooky? Not if I want to pay rent. Broke student, remember?" Her phone chirped again with another notification tone. "Ooh. Look, breaking news from the BBC. They've found the car Prince Ruslan was last seen in right nearby in Rogue. Holy crap."

Holy crap indeed. She'd already mentioned knowing about Prince Ruslan. But thus far my disguise of glasses and the student athlete clothes had worked. It might not hold up if she was staring right at a picture of me. I made like I was grabbing her phone to see the news story and fumbled it right onto the corner of the concrete bench. Crack, the screen shattered. Perfect. "Damn. Sorry, love."

"Oh no. It's a broken mess. Dumb thing. I guess I'll have to go whore myself out to get it fixed tomorrow." She frowned at the thing glumly.

"What?" Was she actually that hard up for money? That must just be an Americanism. "No. It's my fault. Why don't you let me get it fixed and I'll bring it to you at your place of employment?"

Which, of course, I couldn't do with the whole no money, no phone of my own, and no credit cards thing. But I couldn't have her looking up the news about me. Once the one-bloods had been taken care of, I would have a new one sent to her with my apologies. No, better to do that anonymously.

"Is that your sly way of getting my number and asking to see me later? Because I say yes to both." Her smile was as wide as the gap between our two worlds.

I pulled her down for another kiss. "You're quite clever for figuring me out. I definitely want to see more of you."

For a second, I didn't think my wolf would let me let go. I wanted to tug her closer, to mark her, keep her. It took more effort than I was proud of to pry my fingers off her and let her move away.

"Why does everything you say sound both naughty and all proper at the same time?" She nipped at my bottom lip. "Wanna walk me to work? The Wolves' Den is just on the other side of campus."

She had a very cheeky grin that I wanted to look at for a long, long time.

"I'd rather tuck away with you and be as you say, naughty. But I shall pull on every bit of my proper upbringing and escort you to work." I had no desire to do anything but strip her naked and taste every inch of her. I knew I didn't have much time left, but if it meant I got to spend more time with her, I would walk her to Bashkiria and back.

The trip across campus would have to do. It would give me the opportunity to sniff around. Twice already the one-bloods had come for one of the wolves' human mates at the Moon Bean.

It was half of the reason why the Wolf Tzar had called my family in to help. His mother, the Troika matriarch, owned the little shop, and while she had been sly and instrumental in the revolution and take down of the Volkovs, she was only one wolftress. Against a band of thugs, she was a target. As were the women who worked for her.

I nuzzled Stacia's neck before letting her up, and when she stood, I took her hand. I doubted I'd ever get an opportunity to walk hand-in-hand with a sweetheart ever again, and I was going to soak up every bit of a whirlwind romance with my American girl.

$\mathcal{E}$very nerve in my entire body was squealing with delight. Bash kissed me, and then he kissed me again. If my phone wasn't broken and in his pocket, I'd be texting Selena and telling her what an incredibly smart matchmaker she was. I already had to bite the inside of my cheek to keep from awkwardly laughing every time he said anything. Playing it cool, I asked, "How long are you here? One semester or two?"

He took my hand in his as we walked across the main part of campus toward the row of shops and restaurants where the Wolves' Den and the Moon Bean were. "Not long enough, I think."

Be still my heart. Now I really did want to *skive off* so I could spend more time with Bash. It was kind of weird how I felt like we had this instant connection. Yeah, I was beyond attracted to his accent, and I still wanted to see him with nothing but a crown on, but something had happened between us sitting on the benches. Right before he kissed me, when he told me his name, I saw something flash through his eyes. A moment of vulnerability in him that I didn't think he let very many people see.

"I applied for the study abroad program so I could go to Europe and go royals hunting." I hoped he didn't think I was too weird. "Turns out the committee didn't think that was a good reason to want to study in Denmark, Norway, Sweden, the United Kingdom, Spain, the Netherlands, Bashkiria, or Belgium."

He huffed out a half laugh, half cough. "Why those eight countries?"

"Those are the kingdoms left in Europe." He was from there, I would have thought he'd have known. "Princes and dukes and barons and whatnot all over the place. There're also royal families in Andorra, Liechtenstein, Monaco, several African countries, Thailand, and Luxembourg, but none of them have an exchange program with Bay State University."

"I see. So you really have quite a thing for the royals then." He sounded a little disgusted by that.

Very few people understood my obsession. "Ever since I was little. My mom named me after Princess Anastasia and we used to watch the cartoon movie on an old VHS tape she got at a library sale. She even made me a miniature dress-up gown with the big leg-of-mutton sleeves, just like Anastasia's. It's my favorite memory of her."

He gripped my hand tighter. "Memory as in she's not here anymore?"

Usually this conversation was awkward, but with Bash, the words didn't get stuck in my throat waiting for the discomfort from whoever I was talking to. "She died when I was seven."

He stopped us short and turned me to face him. "I'm sorry, love. I can't imagine losing my mother. She's a tough old thing and I think she's decided never to die so I don't have to—" He stopped himself short. "Well, anyway. I'm sorry about your mum."

"Thanks." Most people gave me this kind of condolence by rote, but Bash seemed genuinely sad about it for me. He was sweet and I couldn't believe I was about to say this, but I was falling for him.

No, ridiculous. It was the accent. It had to be. That and the way he kissed, and held my hand, and called me love.

"Is this it?" Bash pointed to the front door of the Wolves' Den.

"Yeah. I'd better hurry in. Don't want to get fired." The last thing I wanted to do was leave his side.

Selena stuck her head out the front door of the bookshop. She gave me a sideways glare, like she was waiting to chastise me about something. Oh. Ha-ha. Her threat about firing me. Well, fire this, Selena.

I grabbed Bash around the neck and laid a big old smooch on him. He wrapped his arms around my waist and gave back as good as he was getting until we were both breathless. Now I really wanted to skip work and drag him back to my place for the night. Ooh. I bet he was good at talking dirty. But to be fair, he could recite Dr. Seuss and I would still get all swoony.

I broke the kiss much sooner than I wanted to, but for real I didn't want to get fired for being late two days in a row. "Come by later for dinner? I don't get off until closing, but I'd love if you were there when I'm done for the night."

"When you're done for the evening, we'll just be getting started." His eyes were dark like a stormy sky and his voice was rough and husky.

Yas. See? Swooning. I touched his lips with a finger just to keep myself from tackling him there on the sidewalk and having my way with him. "See you later."

Later could not come soon enough. But the night flew by,

busy as all get out. Mostly because Ty called in sick. That guy was never ill a day in his life. I'm sure he was in bed, but not with the flu. Unless the flu was also known as his girlfriend, Hunter.

I was excited to see Bash walk in the door late into the dinner rush, but all I could do was wave and blow him a kiss. He figured out pretty quick that I wasn't going to have much time for him. As soon as I could, I popped over to the pool table where he was hanging out with some of the football players.

"Can I get you boys anything?" I asked them all but directed my best smile at Bash.

He licked his lips, and I knew what he really wanted. I mouthed the word 'later' to him.

He grinned and adjusted his glasses. "I'm afraid I'm a bit skint, love."

What? Poor guy couldn't afford a beer? Too bad he hadn't come in on coin night for a quarter beer. "I got you."

He made a funny little face. That was the second time I offered to pay for something for him, and I got the distinct feeling he didn't like it. That gave me a little tickle. Welcome to America. Making independent women, since 1776.

I brought the round of beers the players ordered and set a mug down for Bash too. He shook his head but smiled. As I walked away I heard him say, "You gents in for a game of billiards?"

By the time I made it back to them with another round, Bash laid a twenty-dollar bill on my tray. "That should cover it."

"I thought you didn't have any money." I wasn't going to take his last dollar.

"Your boyfriend here is a shark when it comes to pool. He's won his weight in beer, so I thought it would be easier to pay him off," one of the football guys groaned.

My boyfriend. Is that what he'd told them? I think my heart ka-thumped right out of my chest. "Uh, okay, well, I'll just, uh, be over here... if you need more girlfriends. Ack, I mean drinks."

No one but Bash seemed to notice my verbal diarrhea, and he pursed his lips together like he was trying hard not to laugh. But somehow I knew he wasn't laughing at me, but with me. Gah. I was such a dork.

A dork in love.

As I walked away, one of the football guys started jingling his keys anxiously.

"Hey, I'm just going to check on my bike."

"Why?" Another guy looked up from the shot he was about to take, grinning. "Do you think it ran away?"

"No, jackass. But a lot of cars and bikes have been getting boosted near campus, and I don't want to lose my ride."

It was true. The crime rate had been going up in the area lately. The bikers that had taken to prowling around made it so people didn't exactly feel safe wandering around after dark, and there'd even been a couple break-ins. In a weird way, it kind of made me glad I didn't have a car. And at least the guys were usually willing to walk me to the bus stop after shift.

Finally closing time came, and Liam said he didn't mind if Bash hung out while I closed out the till and bussed the rest of the tables. He'd mentioned something about a hot date and tossed me the keys to lock up.

That left me and Bash all alone. Perfect. "I'll be finished in just a few minutes."

He sauntered over and nuzzled my neck. "You remember what I said about when you were finished?"

Gulp. "Yes."

"Good. But I don't think I can wait that long to get started." Bash pulled me straight into a soul-deep kiss.

I think my toes literally curled up, it was that hot. He backed me up until my butt hit the edge of the pool table. God, it was fricking sexy how he wanted me this bad. Nobody had even looked at me like they wanted me before, much less got all handsy and desperate like what Bash and I were doing at the moment.

I pushed my hands up underneath his sweatshirt and he groaned at my touch. "Your skin is so hot. You're not sick, are you?"

"Every time I touch you, my temperature rises. If I'm sick, I'm sick in love." He tugged at the buttons on my shirt and took my mouth in another kiss.

My tongue was way too busy clashing with his to bother asking him if he meant what he'd said. Could he really be in love with me? It was crazy, right? But if he was crazy, so was I. Two tickets for crazytown, coming up.

Bash grabbed me under the butt and lifted me up to sitting on the edge of the table, easy, like it was nothing. "I can't wait to get you to a bed, Anastasia. I need you too much. Let me take you here and now."

Ooh, he took the words right out of my mouth. I touched the weird green fabric of the pool table beneath my butt. "Liam will kill me if we ruin the pool table."

He shucked his pants and pushed me back onto the table. Then he crawled up and over me like a prowling panther. "I'll buy him a new one."

Wow. Had he won that much money? Also... who cared? I wanted him just as badly. Gone were the fantasies about him wearing a crown and calling me princess while he made love to me. I just wanted Bash, the sweet, adorable glasses wearing, poor, British exchange student who'd somehow captured my heart.

In no time we were both down to our underwear and Bash was nibbling his way across my cleavage. "I want to taste every single inch of your curves and have you screaming my name with my head between your legs."

"Yes, let's do that, but next time. Right now, I want you inside of me. Please." My heart skipped a beat. He needed to know I was a virgin. It was so not fair to keep that from him. God, I hoped he didn't freak out about it, because my vibrator was not going to have enough power to get me through that disappointment.

Here goes nothing, or everything. "Bash, wait. I have to tell you something."

"Anything, love, you can tell me anything and everything. I want to know you inside and out." He punctuated his words with kisses up one side of my neck and down the other.

"I- I mean you, umm... you're my first. I've never done this before, much less on a pool table with a hot British guy who makes my heart go all wobbly." I stopped myself from rambling, but it was a close call.

Bash took a long, slow breath and then looked deep into my eyes. "You are my first too, Anastasia. I had to come all the way across the world to find the right one, and it's you."

Is it possible for a girl to die of swooning? Because I might. "I'm so glad you found me. Took you long enough."

Bash pulled off his glasses and his face lit up with that smile I adored. God, his eyes were beautiful and I could get lost in them. After one day, he was so familiar to me, it was like I'd known him for forever.

He laid the glasses on the pool table and he kissed me deep again and whispered into my ear. "You may be my first, but I will be sure to make sure you're well pleasured, love. No skipping to the me inside of you part."

He licked and kissed his way down my body, nipping and nibbling every inch of me. I pushed my hands into my hair, living in the moment as much as I possibly could. "Feel free to skip those wobbly bit, right there."

"You mean this one right here?" He swirled his tongue around my belly button.

"Uhh." Maybe I was changing my mind about the skipping bits thing. "You'd better do that again, because I'm not sure."

Bash chuckled and did not do as I asked. Instead he took one long lick up the side of my stomach, following the line of the faint lines of my tummy stretch marks. "I'm very turned on by all of your… bits, the wobbly, and the soft, and the rosy pink, and all the rest."

He nibbled his way right between my legs and whooooooo-boy was I wrong about my assumption that vibrators were just as good as the real thing. This wasn't just pleasure, lightning and moonlight and stardust pushed shivers through every cell in my body.

"Bash, you're, oh, god, you're going to make me come." I gripped his hair tight.

His head popped up and he grinned like a loon. A sexy loon. "More than a few times if I'm lucky."

"Wait." I leaned forward and grabbed his face, cupping his cheeks. "I…I want to come with you, together."

He licked his lips, and I swear the gold in his eyes flared, almost like a sunburst trying to get out. "Your wish is my command, my princess."

Princess, huh? It was cute and adorable that he remembered my obsession with them.

"I'll do my best to go slow. Tell me if I hurt you, okay?"

"Okay." I know we were being all honest with each other, but maybe next time I'd tell him that while he was my first lover, there was no way my hymen was intact. Hello… masturbation, party of one. I owned my fair share of vibrators and other sex toys meant for her pleasure. I was a chubby college girl, not dead.

He wasn't going to hurt me, and I couldn't wait to be with

him. I'd never wanted anyone or anything so much in my life, and my body was more than ready for him.

He pushed into me and groaned so deep and low that I felt it in my own chest.

"Fuck, you feel good, Anastasia." He gritted his teeth and his legs shook.

"Don't hold back. You feel just as good to me. I love this, I love you." I wrapped my legs around his hips and pushed my core forward, taking more of him in.

His eyes rolled back and he buried his head in my neck. "Fuck. I want to make you come, but if you do that again, I won't be able to last that long."

I swirled my hips just to see if I could get him to groan like that again. I had a feeling he always had a tight rein on his emotions and even his actions. I wanted to see him let go. For me.

He did.

"Goddess. I am going to fuck you and make you come every day, twice a day, until the day that I die just to get you back for that." Bash thrust into me, and I was the one seeing stars this time. He pumped fast and hard and bit the skin behind my ear.

With each of his thrusts, his body hit me in just the right spots. I'd certainly never found my g-spot before, but he sure as hell did.

"Anastasia, your cunt is gripping my cock so tight, I fucking love it. God, tell me you're close." A sheen of sweat glistened on his chest and throat and I wanted to lick it off him.

"Please don't stop, I'm close too, so close." Tingles raced across my body, ready and waiting to burst from all the excitement and pleasure.

Bash pushed into me fast and hard and kissed me, sucking on my tongue. It was all too much and my body took over, exploding into the best freaking orgasm of my entire life. Bash cried out my name at the same time and his hips jerked, losing his rhythm as he came with me.

There was a sharp pain at my shoulder where Bash had bitten me, but I barely even noticed. But the wave of absolute bliss that came rolling over me, sending me crashing right back into another orgasm that seemed to go on and on and on, now *that* I did notice.

Afterward, I collapsed back onto the pool table, my shoulder throbbing deliciously, my whole body relaxed, with little aftershocks of pleasure zinging along my nerves. I couldn't stop grinning like an idiot.

I couldn't have asked for a better first time. Neither of us were virgins anymore. We'd given that to each other, something we'd never share with anyone else, and that was something special to me.

BASH

*A*nastasia was so much more than I ever expected. Sex with her was not the frolic I'd thought it would be. She meant the world to me. I didn't understand how I could have fallen in love with her practically overnight, but this was so much more than lust. It was for me anyway, and I prayed it was for her too.

Which was a bad thing. I wanted Anastasia in my life, not just for one night, but for a long, long time. That could never happen. Wolves mated other wolves. At least in Bashkiria. My family would not approve of an American human, much less a girl who needed to work for a living.

But I also couldn't give up the throne. I would for her, but that would mean letting my entire country down. I was the last male heir of the Bashkir line. If I didn't assume the throne, there was no one else eligible, no matter how much my scandalous cousins wanted to take their shot. Only male heirs could inherit the pack. Without me, the monarchy of Bashkiria would end.

All things that I would have to think about tomorrow. Tonight, I would hold this lovely woman in my arms and keep her close to my heart. I would need those memories in the years to come when I longed for her while I married another. I would have to provide my own heir.

Fuck.

We were both still breathing hard, and I was still inside of her. I hesitated for a moment. I couldn't pull my cock out. My knot. Holy shit. I was knotted inside of her body. My wolf had chosen her.

I'd bitten her, and knotted her, claiming her as mine, without even realizing it.

Because she was mine. She was my one true mate.

I wouldn't believe it, if anyone had told me I'd find my mate in the States, in a sweet girl with rosy cheeks, and soft glowing skin. But there was no denying. She. Was. Mine.

I could handle anything if it meant I could keep Anastasia at my side. My heart gave an extra thud in my chest. She could be mine forever.

None of that plan was fair to her. She didn't even know who or what I truly was.

An arse is what I was for keeping it all a secret from her. A secret it would remain. She'd be far more upset if she found out my true identity and we never got to see each other again, especially with her adorable obsession with all things royal. No, it was better if she could look back fondly on her one night, if we were lucky two, with the strange British exchange student.

She'd likely be hurt when I disappeared, but less so than if my family and our army of lawyers got involved. They'd offer her money to keep quiet or destroy her. I couldn't let her be hurt that way. I loved her, and for that I would make this sacrifice, even if it made me a miserable sod the rest of my days.

It came back in a rush then. I'd bitten her. I'd marked Stacia, claimed her. I hadn't planned it, hadn't even meant to do it at all, but with her beneath me, so sweet and lush and clinging, my wolf had surged forward, and the next thing I knew my teeth were in her sweet pale pink skin, and she'd been like liquid fire around me.

I hadn't needed the pressure of the knot forming inside her body to prove to me that she was my mate, but I winced at the tug. We were going to be stuck together for a while yet. Luckily, she was sleepy, dozing against me, because I was going to need all the time I could get to figure out how the bloody hell I was going to explain all of it.

In a few hours, the bite would fade, but the mark would form, like a tattoo. Hard to miss, that. I was going to have to think fast.

Though part of me wished I could just… tell her. Everything. About me, about supernatural wolves, about Bashkiria. She'd probably be fine with the royal bit. It was the wolf shifter thing I was worried about.

She was mine, my mate. If my wolf scared her, if she ran from me, I didn't know what I would do. Just the thought of it left me cold.

I grabbed the borrowed sweatshirt to drape over us. It was a good thing I did too.

"Ruslan Bashkir. Get up and put your clothes on immediately, young man." The voice of the Queen of Bashkiria rang through the dirty little bar like a trumpet.

"Fuck."

"Bash?" Stacia looked at me, over at my mother, back at me, and then hid her eyes behind her hand. "Oh my god. Oh. My. God."

"Stacia, I can explain." I reached for her hand, but was yanked off the table by the exact royal guards I had escaped less than forty-eight hours ago. One of them grabbed my pants and threw them at me, hurrying me away from the table. It was a damn good thing that my knot had gone down, or that would have been as painful as it was humiliating.

"Wait, stop. I'm not leaving her like this." I pushed against the guards, but they were easily twice as big as I was and there was no getting through. "Stacia, Anastasia, I love you. No matter what happens, I love you."

I had no idea if she even heard me because I was whisked out through the kitchen and into a waiting limo.

"Put your pants on before your mother returns, your majesty." The captain of the royal guard of Bashkiria rolled his eyes and sighed at me.

Fucking hell. If my family had sent over the captain, I was in a shit ton more trouble than I thought. I yanked my pants on and grabbed a bottle of water from the in-car bar. I was not saying another word until I got to see Stacia again.

I was fully prepared to stick to my guns until my mother got into the limo. She looked me up and down and then waved the captain to get out of the car. Nobody argued with the queen.

I felt like I was six years old and about to be told off for pulling the girl's pigtails. She waited only until the door shut before she laid into me.

"What the hell, Ruslan?" The shake in her voice belied her fear more than her anger. "I was worried out of my mind. I thought you were dead."

"Sorry, Mother." The look on her face had me feeling like a total piece of shite. I hadn't thought about her as my mum in a long time, but she was, even if she put the country first. "I didn't mean to scare you. I just needed some time."

"To sow your wild oats, I see. You know how your father and I feel about sex before mating." Ah, there was the queen again. Now that she knew I was safe and sound, I'd get the tongue lashing I knew was coming all along.

"I do." That's all I had to say about that. I did not want to discuss what had happened between me and Stacia. That was something special for only the two of us.

Best to derail the conversation. "There's been a lot of one-blood activity on campus. I was never going to get close to it as Prince Ruslan, but I've been following the rumors as Bash. They're getting bolder, making challenges."

"All the better to have your guards with you, Ruslan," Mother said, giving me a withering look. "You can't just go haring off to fight those degenerates. If you'd told me, we could have arranged something. What would Bashkiria do if you got hurt?"

What would I do? That was what she didn't say. I stayed quiet, looking out the window of the limo, thinking hard.

"And what are you going to do about this girl then? Pay her off? Leave her to tell her story to the tabloids?" She folded her arms in her usual manner.

"Not this time, mumsie. I think, instead, I'll mate her." It was going to take some sweeping reforms to the culture that ruled the wolves of Bashkiria, but it was time we shook things up, and I was the man to do it. I hadn't known that before this exact moment. I wasn't a mama's boy who always did as he was told, and with this trip to America, the world got to find that out.

I was the future alpha and King of Bashkiria. I would always do what was best for my country and my people, and that meant allowing everyone to choose who they wanted to mate, who made them happy, not stifled by antiquated rules that were really at the root of the miseries we'd suffered. If we weren't free to love and marry the one person right for us, how could we be expected to care about anything else? I was about to change all that.

I expected an angry rebuttal from my mother, but instead she smiled and nodded. "About time you grew up. I told your father a trip abroad was just the thing to shake you up."

It took much longer to get checked into the private boutique hotel and escape the waiting press and paparazzi than I wanted, but by midday, I was showered and changed and headed back to campus, but this time, with a discrete team following me.

I needed to find Stacia. I needed to talk to her. My wolf had surged to the front, prickling against the inside of my skin. The one-bloods were still a threat, getting bolder and harassing the campus. They didn't think highly of humans and had been known to even traffic human women to degenerate packs. And my Stacia was all too human.

The main problem, of course, was that I had no bloody idea where to find her. We'd never made it back to her apartment, and even if I had her phone number, her broken phone was back at my hotel suite.

Without any better options, I headed back to the Wolves' Den, hoping against hope that she might still be there.

The place was all but dead that early in the day, and the fading scent of ripe peaches dashed my hopes thoroughly. She wasn't there.

Ty, one of my fellow Dire Wolves and soon to be alpha of his own newly formed pack, came out of the back with a tub full of clean glasses to start restocking the bar, so I rushed over, practically crossing my fingers.

"Hey, man," Ty greeted me. "What can I get you?"

I raked a hand back through my hair, my wolf all but pacing inside my chest. "Is Stacia here? Anastasia?"

Ty frowned, giving me a look over. "No, sorry man. She called out for the day. Said she wasn't feeling well."

"Ah." Was that because of me? The thought was gutting. "Do you know where she might be?"

Ty gave me another look over, something a little too close to sympathy crossing his face before he shook his head. "Sorry, man."

It had been a long shot anyway. I gave Ty a tight smile and moved away from the bar.

She wasn't there. She was somewhere. My mate was out there, a bunch of one-bloods were circling the campus, and I didn't know where she was or if she was safe.

My wolf surged again, a low snarl building in my throat. I couldn't change, not there, not in broad daylight. The Wolf Tzar would not be amused.

There was one more thing I could try. Bonded mates could share thoughts. It even worked on humans, or at least that was the rumor. If she wasn't too furious at me for lying to her and then leaving her like a cad, even if it hadn't been my choice.

Stacia, I thought, forming the words carefully. *Stacia, where are you? Please, I can explain. Just tell me where you are.*

I waited, barely daring to breathe. A minute passed, and then another.

Stacia?

Every second waiting felt like a knife in the chest.

She didn't answer.

There was only so long I could mope around, at least that was the rumor.

Okay, so the hottest guy I'd ever met, with the yummiest accent, and who had actually made me see stars last night, and into this morning if we're being real, might have secretly been a prince, and he just never bothered to tell me.

I mean, I couldn't blame him after he'd heard me gushing about, well, him. Just remembering how I'd gone on about the royals made me want to crawl into a hole and then pull it shut behind me like something out of a cartoon show.

And then he was gone, poof. Sure, I knew he was an exchange student and that we weren't going to have long together, but that had still been pretty shocking. One second, we'd been cuddling, totally blissed out. The next, the room was full of strangers, one of which might have been Bash's, sorry, Ruslan's mother, the queen.

Thank whatever fates were listening that Bash had thought to toss his sweatshirt over us, or every jiggly inch of me would have been on display in a room full of judgy strangers.

A plate clinked against the table, and I lifted my head out of my arms to Charlize putting some drink that seemed to be at least fifty percent chocolate drizzle and whipped cream in front of me. The Moon Bean's coffee shop was always good for a decadent little pick-me-up.

"Come on, it's not that bad, is it? I mean, nothing's official yet, right?"

I blinked at her, confused. No, Bash and I hadn't been official. I mean, I'd hoped to see him a few more times but… wait, how would Charlize have known that? She hadn't even seen Bash and I together. "Huh?"

Her face contorted into an 'oh crap' expression. "Oh, you, uh, didn't get the alert? I thought that was why you were in mourning over here in the corner."

No, no alert. My destroyed phone was still in the pocket of the crown prince of Bashkiria, which was almost enough to make me laugh, but then I just had to remember him being pulled away from me while I was still naked on a pool table under a sweatshirt, and the urge to laugh died pretty thoroughly.

I hadn't even been home. I meant to, but I just sat in the Wolves' Den, in shock. For hours, I guess, because as the sun rose, I just dragged myself next door to the Moon Bean for coffee and to lick my wounds.

"What alert?"

"Okay, maybe I shouldn't tell you. I mean, if you're already having a bad day and all."

I glared, not in the mood. "Charlize. Just tell me."

She winced and pulled out her phone.

I read the campus alerts that there was a good chance that the queen of Bashkiria's assembly might have to be canceled due to increased crime and violence in the area. Her security team didn't think it was safe for the royals to come to Bay State University.

Well, on one hand, it sucked that the talk was canceled and that my tickets were useless. But, on the up side, it wasn't like I was going to be able to go to the talk anymore. There was no way I could ever be in the same room with someone after they saw me naked on a pool table, huddled under a sweatshirt. I wasn't sure I could be on the same continent, so it was probably for the best that Bash was going back to Europe.

My heart twinged.

I'd thought we were giving each other something, something important. But he'd been lying to me about everything. I guess I couldn't blame him for that. But it still hurt that the last time I was probably going to see him was being ushered out the door and away from me.

Charlize stepped away and took off her apron before sitting across from me. "So if it wasn't the talk, then what's got you so…" She waved a hand, taking in all of me in my moping glory.

"I'm not really up on talking about it right now." I didn't want to think about it. I just needed a little distraction, something to get me out of my funk, so that Bash could move into being a delicious memory.

The bell above the door clanged when Hunter sashayed through the door. She smiled, spotting Charlize, and came right over to crash my little pity party table.

"Hey, are you ready? Hi, Stacia. Are you coming too?"

"Coming where?" It might be the distraction I was looking for, but I wasn't sure my bruised heart was up to hanging out around Hunter and Charlize, both deliriously happy with their gorgeous boyfriends. Hunter was with Ty from work, and Charlize was stupidly in love with her quarterback boyfriend, Eli.

Hunter adjusted her book bag on her shoulder, her curls

bouncing around her face. "We're going to the library to study for the political science exam."

"Actually, that's a good point. You should come, Stacia. It would really help. I suck at that class."

It was one of my better subjects. And at least helping Hunter and Charlize would get my mind off things. It was better than haunting the Moon Bean like I was waiting for Bash to show back up.

"Alright." I tried not to sigh. "Let's go."

As I bent down to grab my bag, I heard Charlize suck in a shocked breath.

I straightened up, looking around. "What? What's wrong?"

Both Hunter and Charlize were staring at me. Well, at my shoulder. I tried to take a look, craning my head, worried I was having some kind of wardrobe malfunction on top of everything else, because wouldn't that just be my luck.

They exchanged a look, doing something complicated with their expressions like they were having a conversation that I couldn't understand.

Hunter's eyebrows shot up, and she bobbed her head in my direction. Charlize cleared her throat and smoothed her shirt down as she turned back to me.

"So, um, Stacia. Did you get a tattoo?"

"What? No." Why would they even ask me that? Who had money for tattoos?

Hunter bounced up onto her toes, a wide grin stretching across her face. "Did you meet anyone… special, lately?"

Thoughts of Bash ran through my head. His accent. His beautiful golden eyes. His adorkable glasses, which, come to think of it, were probably part of his 'not a prince' disguise. And then my thoughts took a hard right turn into the way he'd touched me last night, the strength in his hands when he'd laid me back over the pool table. The way he'd felt moving inside me. Heat rushed into my cheeks.

Hunter squealed. "I knew it!"

"No, no, it's nothing like that." I didn't want them thinking I'd met some amazing guy, because, yes, okay, I had, but it wasn't like I got to keep him. "It's just…"

I couldn't bring myself to say it was nothing. It hadn't been nothing. The connection I'd felt between us, that had been real, and amazing, and there was a good chance that I was never going to see him again.

And then I was blinking hard, trying not to cry. But then I'd just feel pathetic and sad, and I didn't want to be both. "Why did you ask? How did you even know?"

"The claiming mark." Charlize dropped her voice to a whisper, like she was telling me some secret. "We have them too. Who was it? One of the guys from the team?"

I blinked at her like she'd grown a second head. "The what mark?"

They exchanged worried looks.

"Did he not explain it to you?" Hunter bit her lower lip, looking nervous.

My complete lack of sleep last night meant my brain didn't even begin to work out what the heck they were talking about. But whatever it was they were talking around, it seemed like it was maybe a bigger deal than they were trying to let on.

"I actually have no idea what you're talking about. What mark?"

They exchanged another look. Charlize did a little half shrug with one shoulder. "She's going to notice eventually."

Now they were just freaking me out. "Notice what?"

Charlize picked up her phone. "Can you just tug your shirt to the side for a sec? Perfect."

She took a picture and then spun the phone around for me to see.

The skin of my shoulder and neck, which had been bare when I got up yesterday, was suddenly a swirl of ink. A black wolf, howling to the moon and surrounded by a crown, covered the space like the most intricate tattoo I'd ever seen.

"What the hell," I whispered to myself. I yanked at my shirt, craning my head to the side trying to see it for myself. "Where did that even come from?"

Charlize and Hunter stared at each other and then at me. They looked almost as lost as I did.

I hadn't even had anything to drink last night. There was no way I just didn't notice getting a tattoo. I vaguely remembered Bash biting me there, and just the memory of his teeth touching my skin had a warm little shiver running all the way down to my toes.

Okay, cool, cool. New kink unlocked. I hadn't known biting was a turn on. Something to think about when I wasn't freaking out.

Charlize got a look on her face like she was thinking really hard about something. Her brows pinched together, and her gaze was unfocused. I was the one having a mentie B. Maybe it was contagious. Because that was my only explanation for what she was breaking her brain over.

Hunter took my arm and tugged me to my feet. "Okay," she said, way too brightly with way too many teeth in her smile. "Let's go for a walk. We can chat on the way to the library."

I let myself get towed out of the Moon Bean, because why not. What was even my life anymore? Hidden princes, whirlwind romances, and magic tattoos. Whatever.

I barely heard Hunter hiss to Charlize. "What is going on?"

"I don't know," Charlize muttered back. "I'm asking Eli."

I kind of wanted to snap at them that I was having a panic attack, not deaf. But really, yes, my heart was doing a techno impression, and I was confused, and sad, and mad. I was confusmad.

On top of everything, I missed Bash already.

Stacia.

And great. Now I was hallucinating. Because the day wasn't quite trash enough.

Stacia, where are you? Please, I can explain. Just tell me where you are.

Sure. Why not? I was hearing voices. Because that might as well happen.

Stacia?

As if Bash would sound that sad and apologetic. He was the one who left me. And didn't mention that he was a prince.

A lump formed in my throat, and I shook it off, and just let the girls drag me along toward the campus library.

BASH

*I*n three days, I'd crossed an ocean, come to a foreign country, met the woman destined by fate to be mine, discovered the glory of her body and what we could have together, and lost her. It was an impressive cock up, even in my family. It was like I'd watched the example of my scandal-loving cousins, and then decided to do a more impressive job on a speed run.

Bollocks.

I couldn't find Stacia, I had no way to contact her.

She wasn't answering me across the bond that had formed when I'd claimed her, which, of course, I'd never gotten the chance to explain to her at all.

I could still feel her if I closed my eyes and held my breath. Just a flutter of awareness, enough to know that she was still in the area and safe, though upset. And who could bloody blame her for that?

It would have been one thing to have a whirlwind romance with a gorgeous American bird. Sow my oats, as they say, leave her with a smile and some fond memories. But the idea of never seeing Stacia again, it had my wolf threatening to burst out of my skin to track her down the old-fash-ioned way.

And wouldn't that just be the cherry on top, ambushing her as an enormous wolf. Because I hadn't quite done enough screwing things up yet.

I had a choice to make, search for Stacia directly, with very few clues, or perhaps seek out my new friends on the Dire Wolves football team. While they knew me by reputa-tion, a few short days might be too soon to truly call them friends. I wasn't sure I'd trust them so quickly if the situation were reversed.

Because of course, I also hadn't made any progress on tracking down the one-bloods. They were making their presence felt around the campus, but they didn't exactly hang about. I knew I was on the right track, just like I'd told Mother, but actually being able to catch up to them wasn't working out as well as I'd hoped.

So, all in all, my trip so far was a royal cock up.

No, I wouldn't say that. If I hadn't come to Bay State University, I'd have never met Stacia, and I would have gone on being a miserable sod, never knowing what I was missing out on.

It was just hard to keep that in mind when I couldn't bloody find her. Some tracker I was.

I'd ended up just wandering the campus, trying to catch a whiff of delectable ripe peaches or to stumble across some one-blood plot in the act, and that was going about as well as the rest of my day had, baring a few far too short hours with my gorgeous mate., giving her all the orgasms she wanted, and then more.

"Hey, Bash."

Few enough people knew that name that I actually dragged myself up out of the impressive bout of brooding I had going on in time to see Stone Silver making his way across the quad toward me.

We'd hit it off rather well in my time at Bay State, however brief it had been. He was a bit of a fish out of water too. Recruited from somewhere out in Colorado to be a Dire Wolf and as an extra set of fangs to handle the one-bloods. Apparently the Silver pack out there grew them big, because Stone was bloody huge.

It had been nice though. The other Dire Wolf players had mostly all known each other for years now. Having another new bloke around, we'd kind of ended up gravitating toward each other, and I hadn't realized how much I'd missed having a pack around me until I'd showed up for football practice.

Not all the players were werewolves, but enough of them were. It had helped keep me steady. We tend to form groups by nature, and true lone wolves can go a bit odd if they're alone for too long. They can get mean without the bonds to help. Of course, a bad bunch can go mean too, depending on who their alpha is. Just look at the one-bloods.

Stone hitched his bag a bit higher up on his shoulder, tree trunk legs eating up the distance between us, and I waited for him to catch up.

He gave me a look, his brow furrowed. "You good?"

And wasn't that the bloody question? I prodded at the mate bond in my head again, trying to glean some hint of where Stacia might be or with who. But other than the vague echo that she was alright, or at least not in immediate danger, there was nothing.

No. I wasn't good. Not by a long shot.

"I don't know how to answer that," I admitted, and it was probably the most honest thing I'd said since I set foot in this country.

Stone didn't make a joke or push me to talk. I got the feeling it wasn't really his way, and that was probably why we'd gotten on so well. He just fell into step beside me, following the aimless path I'd been walking. He'd told me that he was one of five brothers and that someone was always talking, so he'd just kind of fallen into place as the quiet one out of self-defense for his ears.

"Do you believe in fated mates?" I blurted out, and then sincerely thought about kicking myself in the arse.

Stone gave me a look like I was crazy, which I probably deserved.

"Yeah. Of course."

That hadn't been the response I'd been expecting. In Bashkiria, the idea of having one perfect fated mate was a fairy tale, something children might believe in. We mated for alliances and political gain. I'd assumed that was what I'd be going home to when my assignment was done. Some done-up aristocrat that my parents had picked out.

But that was before I'd known Stacia was *mine*. I'd bitten her. I'd claimed her. I'd held her in my arms as she writhed and gave that little hitching cry and came around my cock. The idea of letting her go, just going home and marrying some other wolftress, it made my stomach clench like I was going to be sick.

No. It wasn't going to happen. I owed my people a good queen, and Stacia would be exactly what we needed. I'd make whatever reforms were necessary, I'd fight the entire bloody parliament if I had to. Mother had already agreed, and with her backing, I could do anything.

Anything except find my mate, tell her how I felt, and oh yes, let her know that I was a bloody werewolf.

What if she didn't take it well? What if she was frightened, ran from me? It wasn't as though I'd done anything to inspire her trust. I hadn't even been honest about who I bloody was.

But, even as royal mad as she was, she hadn't looked at me

and seen Prince Ruslan. She'd just seen Bash, and she'd decided that was who she wanted.

There weren't many women in the world that wanted me just for me. I was one lucky fool that fate had pushed her into my path.

It would be nice if it could give us another little nudge now.

Stone was still quiet, just walking beside me, content to let me stew. His easy presence was what let me finally spit out the fears tearing me up like a claw from the inside out.

"I fucked up. I fucked up so hard, I don't even know if I can fix it."

Stone stayed quiet, but it was obvious he was still listening.

"I found my mate. I didn't think she existed, but I found her. And I claimed her."

A smile broke out over Stone's face, and he thumped me on the back hard enough that a human probably would have ended up eating dirt.

"That's great. Happy for you, man."

And for that second, I was happy too. Remembering Stacia's laugh, how soft her skin was, all her bloody gorgeous curves.

And then it all crashed back to earth.

"Yeah. Thanks. Except she's human, I lied to her about who I was, and she still doesn't know I'm a wolf."

Stone winced.

"And because, of course, if I'm going to bollock up my entire life, I'm going to do a right proper job of it, I claimed her and then got dragged away, literally, and left her there."

Stone sighed. "Dude."

"And now I can't find her. I don't have her number, I don't know where she lives, so I'm just wandering around like a useless tit and hoping I'll get the chance to see her again before I end up leaving the bloody country."

No. I wouldn't be leaving. Not until I'd seen her. Unless Stacia told me to my face to leave her, it wasn't going to happen.

"We could go hunt something."

It was such an odd thing to say that I tripped. "What?"

Stone shrugged. "Just head to the woods, change, hunt something down. My mother always took apologies better with food."

"She's human. Human women don't usually like gifts of dead animals."

Stone frowned. "Yeah. That does make it harder."

"Besides," my fingers curled into fists, claws pressing at the tips from the inside, "there's only one thing I want to hunt right now."

That made Stone crack a smile, one that had a few too many sharp teeth in it. "A gift of a mangled one-blood probably wouldn't go over well with a human woman either."

I almost laughed. But then a wave of icy terror slammed into me across the bond, and it nearly sent me to my bloody knees.

Stacia.

She was in danger.

"I'm coming, my heart. I will find you."

Normally, I really liked the campus library. It didn't have the caffeine and goodies of the Moon Bean, but it was quiet, and it had all kinds of nooks to hole up in and do some research or catch up on the latest royal gossip going on in the world. The library was kind of secluded, off to the side of the campus, surrounded by trees, a hidden little gem, with the big bronze statue of Bay State's Dire Wolf out in front.

I just couldn't really get into the feel of a good cram session though. I was still trying to wrap my head around where the heck the tattoo on my neck had come from. Having to walk past the snarling statue out front didn't exactly help.

The second we hit the old red brick building, I dove into the bathroom and wrenched the neck of my sweater off my shoulder.

I mean, I hadn't thought that Charlize was pranking me with some new photo filter, but I had to check just to be sure. There it was, right on my skin, the wolf howling to the moon surrounded by an ornate crown. I'd never seen a tattoo so detailed. I half expected the ink to move, like the wolf's fur might rustle in the breeze.

It didn't wash off, and even when I scrubbed at it, it just turned my skin pink and rosy. And I wasn't an expert, but weren't new tattoos kind of gross? All puffy and swollen? Because my ink was perfect, like I'd just been born with this wolf mark on my neck.

Eventually, Charlize barged into the bathroom and dragged me out.

"Okay, no freaking out. I get it, but just try to relax for a second."

I gave her the wide-eyed look that comment deserved.

"Yeah, fair." She tugged me toward the front desk. "Try anyway."

Hunter had stopped at the desk to nag at the girl working there, and in the time I'd been having my little bathroom meltdown, it looked like she'd managed to pry the librarian away from the book she was reading.

"Come on, Eva," Hunter whisper-shouted. "I know not all the rooms are in use."

Eva sighed and flipped her book closed. "You know you're supposed to reserve them in advance, right?"

"It's kind of important. And you're my cousin. Let's do that nepotism thing."

Eva shook her head but swung her chair around to the old boxy computer at the desk. A few clicks later, she turned back. "Okay, room 2C is yours for two hours."

Hunter grinned. "You're the best!"

I was still shellshocked enough that they managed to drag me up the stairs and into one of the private study rooms. They were usually used for group meetings so that people wouldn't disturb everyone else in the building by being loud. There was a table, some reasonably comfortable chairs, and a big window looking out over the campus.

I glanced out the window, and I couldn't help staring at the wolf statue. Sometimes, for homecoming and stuff, the football team and cheerleaders would come and decorate the statue. Just looking at it had my hand creeping up to press over the mark on my neck again.

"Okay, look." Charlize tugged my hand away. "You didn't have that mark yesterday. So how about you walk me through your evening, and maybe Hunter and I can explain a few things."

Sure, this might as well happen. It wasn't like I wasn't planning on dishing with Charlize and Hunter, it was just that I was hoping to have more than one night to squee about.

"Um, so, you know that guy that I ran into at the Moon Bean? Literally. And Selena told me to chase after him and kiss him? Well, mission accomplished. Guess I get to keep my job now."

Hunter's eyes had started to sparkle, and Charlize cackled. "Yes, get yours! And then what?"

"Um, we ran into each other again, and I told him to meet me after work, and we spent the night together." Not even a night, but a few moments. Precious, delicious moments.

It seemed so clinical, saying it like that. It had been so hot and so special, and every time Bash touched me, it had felt like my skin was going to split open and let something shining and glowing and golden spill out. Just thinking about it, about the things he'd whispered in my ear in that accent, had me squirming in my seat.

Charlize, the one out of group who'd had a smexy Dire Wolf boyfriend the longest, grinned at me. "Good?"

"Oh, holy heck, yes." I clapped my hands over my face, trying to hide both the blush flooding my cheeks and the grin that threatened to split my face in half. Remembering how it all ended did a good job of throwing a bucket of water on the smoldering ashes though.

"Um, he got called away though." No way was I telling them about being burst in on by his mom, the queen. That was my personal nightmare fuel. "And I don't have his number. Or know where he lives. And, um, I don't think he's coming back."

The words sank in my gut like a stone in a deep well. I didn't think he was coming back. And I'd known that what time we had together was going to be super short, but I guess I'd thought at least a few more hours.

"Oh, he's coming back alright," Charlize muttered.

I frowned at her. "Why would you say that?"

"Never mind." Hunter cut in. "Did your guy happen to bite you in the middle of things?"

Okay, what the heck? "How could you possibly know that?"

Hunter ignored my question. "And he didn't mention anything? Anything, maybe, unusual about himself? Maybe something that you thought was a joke or a line you didn't understand?"

What the heck was she talking about? "No? He… we didn't really get a chance to talk about much."

Okay, that hadn't come out right. But I didn't regret grabbing for a bit of happiness when it fell into my lap. Whatever else happened, I'd gotten to spend a freaking amazing night with a really amazing guy.

Who'd lied about who he was. Or, at least, heavily edited. But then, I probably never would have gotten to meet Prince Ruslan, not like I had Bash. So I couldn't even really be mad at him for that.

Hunter looked frustrated. She and Charlize had another of those silent conversations that seemed to be made mostly out of eyebrow motions and rolled eyes.

"Okay, not loving the super-secret meeting you're having while in the same room as me, guys."

"No, sorry, it's just…" Charlize made some vague hand gestures. "We're not sure how much we're allowed to tell you."

"Allowed to tell me?" Saying the words back to them slowly didn't actually help.

"That, and we don't want to freak you out," Hunter chimed in.

"Yeah, that ship sailed, crashed, and sank to the bottom of the ocean already."

Charlize made a sympathetic little pout. "Just know that we one hundred percent believe that your guy will be coming back to you. And try to keep an open mind."

"Oh, yeah, that's good advice." Hunter grinned. "This is going to be so exciting."

My head hurt. I was tired. The delicious aches from last night were starting to fade into just the regular kind, and I wanted to go home, eat some ice cream, and drown myself in my new romance novels. And if I started imagining Bash in the place of every book boyfriend in the pile, well, no one had to know it but me.

"I'm sorry, guys. I don't think I'm up for a study session. Maybe tomorrow, if you can meet before work."

The sudden roar of an engine outside made me almost jump out of my skin. A chorus of woops and howls tore through the late afternoon, and we all ran to the window to see what the heck was going on.

There were a bunch of jerks on motorcycles out in front of the library, bringing their bikes up onto the sidewalk, circling on the lawns and tearing up the grass as they went. They looked like bikers too. Big guys, though some of them were more lanky than anything, dressed in leather jackets and no helmets.

There was something written on the back of their jackets, and I squinted to make out the words. Fur and Fangs? Weird name for a motorcycle group.

One of them had something like a baseball bat, and as he drove by, he took a swing at the Dire Wolf statue on the green. A hollow boom echoed across the campus as the bat hit home, and he cackled and drove on, leaving one bronze ear curled in.

I sucked in a shocked breath, seeing red. The Dire Wolf was our mascot, the pride of the school. Who the heck did those jerks think they were?

I grabbed my bag and bolted out of the room, heading for the stairs. Hunter and Charlize were hot on my heels, but I couldn't hear what they were saying over the pounding of blood in my ears.

There was a crowd of people all bottled up in the doorway, trying to see what was going on. Eva hung back, looking unsure, until Professor Rojo came striding out of one of the side rooms, an impressive scowl twisting his face.

"What is going on here?"

No one had a chance to answer him before another chorus of howls and shouts rose up outside. Professor Rojo pushed his way through the crowd, his face grim. He turned, glancing through the faces until his gaze landed on Eva.

"Take everyone to the back of the building, away from the windows. No one goes outside until I give the all clear, understand?"

Eva mostly looked relieved to have someone with a plan, and she started ushering everyone away. The crowd left, moving deeper into the library.

Charlize had that odd, faraway look on her face again. She stared out the windows like she was looking at something very different. When she spoke suddenly, I jumped.

"Eli is on his way."

I frowned at her. "Did you call him? Is it safe for him to come here? I mean, those guys look like bad news."

Professor Rojo snorted, looking unimpressed. "One-bloods always are."

Hunter, wide-eyed, flapped her hands at him while Charlize made a slashing gesture across her own throat with her hand. Professor Rojo gave them a baffled look.

I glanced between them, feeling like everyone was reading from a different thriller novel or something than I was. "Um, what's a one-blood?"

Professor Rojo turned that baffled look toward me.

"Hey, Stacia, maybe we should go with the others." Hunter tugged at my arm, smiling nervously.

A bottle flew through the air and smashed against the wall beside the window, making all of us jump. Well, not Professor Rojo. He just looked irritated, like a biker gang was a mild inconvenience.

A few of the other bikers had started taking swings at the Dire Wolf statue as they road by, tearing up the grass.

"Shouldn't we stop them? Can someone call the police?" My phone was busted, so even if Bash hadn't taken it, I still wouldn't have been able to call anyone.

Still, it was a good plan. We could call campus security, or better yet, the actual cops, and they could come and handle things. I started to turn toward the front desk where they had a land line set up, when I caught sight of one biker out of the corner of my eye.

He was a big guy, with a heavy beard and a swagger like he was the biggest, toughest thing to ever walk the world. He strutted up to the Dire Wolf statue, and what he had in one hand had a bolt of icy panic shooting up my spine.

It was a hacksaw.

He set the teeth against the Dire Wolf's bronze neck like

he was going to take the whole head off, and something in my chest popped like a water balloon.

I was so sick of these guys, with their intimidation and stealing from people. They'd made me feel unsafe on campus, and they got the royal talk, maybe my one last chance to see Bash, canceled. And now they wanted to deface our mascot? Our pride?

I wasn't really sure what I was doing when I stormed out the door, shaking off Charlize and Hunter's hands. But I knew I couldn't just stand by and watch.

My heart was pounding the second I set foot outside. It was nuts. What was I doing? But something I really didn't understand, some force inside me, had its hackles raised and its teeth barred at just the sight of those bikers. How dare they come here and start trouble on my campus?

A couple of the bikers rolled to a stop, their heads tilted back, and it looked almost like they were sniffing the air, which was super weird. One of them turned to glance in my direction, and the look he gave me, eyeing me like a piece of meat… in a pie shop made me want to take a bath.

He gave a sharp whistle, and all the others stopped what they were doing and turned in my direction.

Having all their attention on me made me want to turn and run back into the library. Maybe hide under one of the desks. But the same feeling that had driven me out the door in the first place wouldn't let me bolt. I was freaked out, but I still tipped my chin up and stared the bikers down.

"Get out of here. You don't belong here."

The big bearded guy actually laughed at me, and the others joined in pretty quickly. He looked me over again, a disgusting leer on his face. He opened his mouth to talk— and say something slimy I was sure—but then his gaze landed on my neck.

Or on the tattoo that was peeking out above my stretched-out collar.

The biker guy's face twisted with fury, red creeping up his neck and into his face. "Look at that. Even the old bloodlines are slumming it with human trash. They aren't even wolves anymore. Just dogs."

My heart was slamming against my ribs and my stomach felt like someone had tied a cinder block to it and dropped it off the pier, but I wasn't going to cower. Hopefully someone had taken my advice and called the cops.

Professor Rojo stepped out beside me, adjusting his cuffs like he was about to give a lecture.

"You heard the lady," he said. "Get lost."

Well, none of them liked that. A weird tension rolled through the group of bikers, and they stared at the professor with something very close to hate.

"You don't tell us what to do, you overgrown lizard. We're taking back what's ours."

The biker leader's head swung back to me while I was still mouthing a confused lizard to myself. His look had my mouth snapping shut so fast my teeth clicked together.

"And we're going to show those weak, pathetic dogs why you don't mate with human trash."

I didn't even have a chance to get angry about any of that, because a second later, the biker guy fell forward with a bunch of ugly, cracking pops. The bones of his face shifted around, and ratty, gross hair grew over his arms, and the snarl he gave me had about a hundred too many teeth, all of them long and way, way too sharp.

Oh.

Okay.

So this was what a psychotic break felt like. Cool.

Cool. Cool.

I was moving before I even fully understood what was going on. All I knew was that Stacia, my mate, was terrified, and I wasn't there beside her, and that was enough to have my wolf throwing itself against the cage of my body.

Stone had burst into a run when I did, keeping pace. "What is it? What's going on?"

I didn't know. I didn't know where she was, but I had to *go*, I had to find her. I tried to tell him that, but all that came out was a guttural snarl.

Stone's head cocked to the side as we ran. "Hear that?" he asked, grim. "Motorcycles on campus."

Most students didn't ride on the campus, which meant that there was a good chance it was the one-bloods kicking up trouble again. It was a chance for me to finally catch at least one of them, who could hopefully lead me back to whoever was behind their group.

But Stacia was in trouble. I'd burn the bloody world for her. It wasn't even a choice.

Of course, there was a chance that they were the trouble she was in. Not knowing was going to drive me mad.

As we raced past the gym, a crowd of our fellow Dire Wolves came pelting out, with Eli in the lead and Ty close on his heels. Nik was with them, and Kirill, and a few others whose names I couldn't remember past the driving beat of Stacia's fear.

"What's going on?" Stone called to the others.

"One-bloods, at the library," Eli said, shortly. "Charlie's there, and I'm not letting one of those pricks lay a finger on her."

"Is Stacia with her?" I almost didn't recognize my own voice. The question came out as more of a growl than words.

Eli nodded, his face grim. "Yeah. Hunter too. And a bunch of humans."

That was all I needed to hear. My Stacia, my gorgeous American girl, was in the same vicinity as a bunch of one-bloods.

I leapt forward and let the wolf out.

Clothing tore, and wasn't that going to be a bugger later. But I didn't care. Just like I didn't care about the voices calling behind me. There was nothing but the grass moving beneath me as I raced to close the distance.

I heard the soft thudding of feet coming up beside me and risked glancing back just enough to see an enormous white wolf keeping pace. Stone.

A wolf's body isn't really meant for nodding or anything human like that, but I flicked my ears toward him, glad for the backup.

The wolf was far faster than the man, and just a few seconds later, we tore across the green to the library's secluded courtyard. There was a whole pack of one-bloods there, and one of them had even started to shift, his skin splitting and his bones cracking, before we'd gotten there. He was a big hulking brute, snarling at the small woman standing on the front steps, her eyes wide and her skin soft, pale, and glowing in the moonlight.

Glowing for me.

Stacia.

Something in me soared at the sight of her but crashed back to earth a second later to realize that my mate was alone, undefended except for... strangely a dragon, masquerading as a professor standing beside her as she faced down an enormous werewolf, her book bag clutched in her hands like a sword.

The one-blood lunged forward, and I put on another burst of speed, knowing I wasn't going to get there in time.

A book came sailing out the door of the library to slam into the one-blood's head and knock it to the side with a furious snarl. From inside the library came a woman's happy little, "Yes!" and then a hail of books came raining down on the one-bloods assembled there.

I didn't care. They could have dropped a house on the grass. All that mattered was that it distracted the shifted one-blood long enough for me to catch up.

It was time to show those disgusting upstarts just how we did things in Bashkiria.

I slammed into his side with a furious snarl, laying in with teeth and claws. Like all cowards when faced with a serious opponent, the one-blood tried to bolt. I let him go after giving him a good bite across the shoulder to remember me by. I had bigger things to worry about.

Then, finally, Stacia was there, staring at me with wide eyes.

Because I was a wolf.

I froze. Would she scream? Would she run? Did she see me as an animal? A monster? It felt like someone had scooped out my guts and replaced them with concrete.

But she just swallowed hard and licked that perfect, plump bottom lip of hers.

"Bash?"

My heart leapt. She knew me. She *saw* me. My mate wasn't afraid, not of me. I wanted to throw my head back and give thanks to the Goddess.

"Bash, look out!"

I felt the rush at my back and twisted to the side, sinking my fangs into the one-blood who'd tried to ambush me.

The rest of the Dire Wolves burst onto the scene, and the rest of the one-bloods all either decided to ditch their human forms or make a run for it. Stone laid into the leader, snarls ripping through the air as fur flew. Ty and Eli made for the library, until two faces appeared in the window and the girls started waving.

That explained the rain of books then.

The pair of them didn't waste any more time, bursting free in a wave of fur and fangs and throwing themselves into the fight.

I gave Stacia a quick once-over, checking for injuries, but I didn't scent any blood. Just the faintest hint of ripe peaches that I'd been afraid I might never smell again.

I turned back to the one-blood under my claws.

My mate was there, and she wasn't afraid of me. What was a fight with a bunch of pathetic excuses for werewolves compared to that? I could do bloody anything, so long as Stacia was with me.

kay.
So.

Things happened pretty quickly, and my whole head felt a bit like an etch-a-sketch. Like, when I'd woken up yesterday morning, there had been two things that I'd known for sure. That I was going to go to law school, and that freaking werewolves didn't exist.

Standing there on the front steps of the library, it felt a bit like someone had come along and given me a few hard shakes, and I had to fiddle with the knobs and redraw some lines.

When the biker guy had suddenly turned into a monster movie nightmare and then a huge black wolf had come thundering across the lawn toward him, I should have freaked. Like, just screamed and run for it. But I hadn't.

Because when the second wolf had turned its beautiful dark head toward me and I'd looked into those huge golden eyes, all I'd seen was Bash.

When I'd called his name, his ears had perked up, and if that wasn't the cutest freaking thing. Which then made me feel a bit crazy, because there was literally a werewolf fight happening less than twenty feet from me, and I was cooing inside my head about how sweet Bash's ears were.

Priorities.

More and more of the bikers were changing, and one of them took the chance to throw themselves at Bash's back, and I yelled out a warning.

Bash stepped to the side, moving more like a shadow than an animal, and he'd snatched that werewolf right out of the air and thrown it onto the steps, where it landed with a pained yelp.

And that was when everything had gone totally off the rails.

Because a big chunk of the football team had shown up, including Hunter and Charlize's boyfriends, and then they'd all started turning into wolves too.

And then, if that wasn't all bonkers enough, Professor Rojo stepped forward and red scales started flowing up his neck and across his face, and he grew a snout. His whole head was replaced by what looked like a dragon's head, and when one of the still-human-looking bikers charged with a length of pipe in his hand, that long snout opened, and he just breathed fire all over the place.

All I could do was stare, watching black flakes of ash rain down onto the grass like really gross snow.

I just... wasn't going to think about that. It was hard to ignore, with the dragon man literally standing next to me, but I'd gotten really good about compartmentalizing bad memories and scary things, and I distracted myself by watching Bash.

I knew he was hot, I mean, really hot. Smoking hot. With the eyes, and the face, and the body, and... anyway. But he was beautiful as a wolf too. He flowed through the fight, moving so fast and so gracefully, just managing to never be where the biker wolves' teeth snapped shut.

One of them tried sneaking up behind him, and I bent down to pick up one of the books that Charlize had thrown and whipped it as hard as I could. It made a really satisfying thwack when it smacked into the biker's skull.

And then, because this wasn't a weird enough episode of the Twilight Zone yet, with werewolves and dragon men and magic tattoos, some cars screeched up the path between the buildings, and a bunch of men in dark suits came pouring out.

I knew the gossip rags were right about the Men in Black.

"Are they the secret service?" Charlize called to Hunter, and I had to admit they did kind of look like government officials, except they only seemed interested in fighting their way to Bash's side.

The royal guard, I realized with a jolt. Because Bash was a prince. A werewolf prince.

I almost laughed.

The men in suits pretty much all just exploded right out of their clothes and turned into wolves themselves, and they joined the fight. With Professor Rojo barbequing any bikers that got a little too close, the ones that hadn't just run off were pretty quickly captured. Several of the royal guardsmen shifted back into their human forms, their very naked human forms, and bundled the unconscious bikers into the back of one of the cars.

And then I lost track of what everyone else was doing, because the beautiful black wolf that Bash had become was trotting toward me, and then with a pop and a weird slide of skin, Bash was there, in my arms.

He pulled me into his chest, clutching a little too tightly as he rained kisses down onto my head.

"Stacia, Stacia, my Stacia. I've been looking everywhere. I'm so sorry, love."

He pulled me a little tighter into his chest. His bare chest. Because Bash was totally and utterly naked, and that was distracting enough that I had to jerk my thoughts back into line to even hear what he was saying.

When he finally let up enough for me to breathe, I leaned back enough to see his face. "So. A prince, huh?"

He winced. It was so much easier to see without the glasses. I felt like a bit of a dope. I was never going to make fun of Lois Lane again for not recognizing Superman in his Clark Kent disguise.

"Among… other things."

Yeah, fair. The werewolf bit was at least as surprising as the hidden royalty bit. I realized I was stroking his chest and made myself stop, because it was really distracting.

"I… have so many questions."

"And I will answer all of them, love. I promise. But I have to go."

I jerked in his arms. "Wait, what? Go?"

And I realized then that the royal guards were fanned out, covering their naked junk, clearly waiting for their prince.

"I need to take the one-bloods to the Wolf Tzar for inter-rogation. They have information that I made a promise I'd find out." He flashed his teeth in something that was a little too feral to be a smile. "But the second that's done, I will be with you. I promise."

I was ready to be upset, maybe even angry, but then Bash's mouth was on mine, lips and teeth and tongues clashing like he was starving for the taste of me, and heat was roaring through my body and my knees turned to water. I had to cling to his shoulders just to keep from ending up a puddle of goo on the ground.

When we finally broke apart and I had enough air to speak, I managed a very small, "Okay."

One of the guards, who must have come prepared with a change of clothes because he was the only guy not naked, came forward to drape a coat over Bash. That was a crime, hiding all that gorgeous brown skin.

Bash made his way to the car, but he never once took his eyes off my face, like he was afraid I'd disappear if he looked away. I felt the same, so I couldn't exactly judge.

I felt that golden gaze on me, right up until the car turned the corner and disappeared.

My shoulders slumped.

"Are you okay?" Charlize laid a hand on my shoulder, and I managed a shaky nod.

"Well, we're not going to be," Hunter hissed, looking terrified. "Help me pick up these books and get them back inside before Eva sees. You think werewolves are scary? That's nothing on a furious librarian!"

Charlize winced but started gathering books. "Come on, Stacia. We can talk while we work. We have a lot to tell you."

BASH

It almost killed me to leave Stacia there, but an interrogation was no place for her to be. She was brave, she hadn't flinched even once, not from the one-bloods and not from me, but there were just some things I didn't want her to have to deal with.

But I was going to have to make things up to her in a big way. From leaving her the first time, even though it hadn't been my idea, to not telling her what and who I was before I claimed her as my mate, and for having to leave her there on the steps of the library to carry out my duty.

I had a pretty good idea on how to do it too.

It didn't take long to find out what the one-bloods knew, however little that was. But at least that group wouldn't be harassing the BSU campus any longer, so that was something.

There was, of course, the formality of delivering the information to Nikolai Troika, the Wolf Tzar who had recently risen to power, and after a brief pause to clean up and attempt to make myself presentable after a whirlwind few days, Mother and I were on our way to the speaking engagement at the student center at Bay State University as originally scheduled.

It had taken a bit of finagling, but I'd gotten my royal guards on board with my plan. A couple of phone calls to the press promising them the royal story of the century helped too.

When the president of the university announced my name and the crowd in the auditorium clapped, I was ready to rock and roll, as the Americans say. I stepped up to the podium, and right there, front and center where I'd insisted she be escorted, was Stacia. My heart pounded hard in my chest, and for one moment, I forgot how to breathe.

She was breathtaking. She was also miffed as hell. I hoped I would get to see both over and over again for the rest of my life. Hopefully less of the being miffed bit though. Becoming a princess should help improve her mood.

I had a speech all prepared for me by the press secretary, and I crumpled it up. I spoke directly into the microphone while looking down at Stacia. Cameras flashed, the audience went quiet, and the room disappeared for me.

It was only her and me in this great big world.

"I am sorry I didn't tell you who I was. You see, my parents are quite the sticklers when it comes to pre-marital relations. They are of the firm belief that one should only engage in sexual congress with the one person to whom they shall marry." The cameras clicked and flashed, the film rolled. Soon all the world would know who and what I was. A man in love.

Stacia narrowed her eyes, looked around at the people seated near her who were all staring, and the cameras pointed at her face. With a frown and a shrug, she ignored them like I was doing. She sat back in her chair like this was the most casual of conversations. "That's pretty old school."

At least she was talking to me. That was all I needed.

"That phrase describes my entire family to a tee. But now that I've met you, I think I agree with my mother all the same."

Stacia stood up and put her hands on her hips. "Are you trying to say we shouldn't have slept together?"

Murmurs rippled through the crowd, and I could physically feel the excitement pouring off the reporters. They thought they were in for a scandal and they loved nothing better.

Stacia didn't stop there, and her fire had me getting hard for her all over again. She waved a hand around, talking loud enough for everyone to hear. "Because I reject that outright. I'm pretty mad at you, but I also am kind of in love with you. So there."

That's all I needed to hear. I'd known it in my heart, but those words from her lips gave me that last bit of strength I needed to throw off the cares of being a royal prince and become her lover.

I jumped down off the stage and pulled her into my arms. "No, my adorable American, I'm saying I want you to marry me. I'm in love with you too. Anastasia, will you be the next Princess Bashkir, future Queen of Bashkiria?"

I couldn't hear her answer over the eruption of cheers from the crowd, but her smile and the way she kissed me gave the answer I wanted.

When the crowd died down, I pulled her up onto the stage and waited for the onslaught of questions from the press. Stacia handled them in her adorable American way.

"Anastasia, Anastasia, over here. Do you have any royal blood in your family?"

Uh-oh. Here came the unanswerable questions. Stupid press would, of course, glom onto that first instead of our obvious happiness.

She shook her head. "Nope. I do not have an ounce of blue blood in me. It's all-American red."

"Then how can you be a princess?" another reporter asked.

"Uhh…"

I was prepared to step in and tell the press about my plans to reform the Bashkirian laws, but Stacia winked at me and pulled the mic closer to herself. "Princess of Bashkiria says what? What?"

I laughed out loud and dipped her down, kissing her long and hard for all of them to see. I might be the blue blood, but she was my beating heart.

EPILOGUE: STACIA

uture Princess of Bashkiria. I still couldn't believe it. That so wasn't me. I wasn't sure I even could be.

Sure, every little girl hopes to meet Prince Charming and have him whisk her off to the big, beautiful castle, but that's not real. There are rules that govern who royals can and cannot marry. I should know, I'd studied them. Being pre-law had to come in handy sometime.

While I was ready to go to Yale Law on a full-ride scholarship in the fall, what I apparently wasn't good at was investigations. I couldn't believe I hadn't recognized Bash as Ruslan Bashkir. But now I totally understood how Clark Kent had fooled Lois Lane. Those glasses, man.

I practically vibrated through the rest of the impromptu press conference and then Bash's speech about how our generation needed to get involved in global political reform. That wasn't what he'd been scheduled to talk about and god, I found his smarts super sexy. Why didn't he let people see this side of him more often instead of the bachelor playboy from Bashkiria? Though I understood why he kept the whole werewolf thing out of the tabloids.

Charlize and Hunter sat me down after the whole library showdown and had given me a talk that they called 'Werewolf Mates 101', and I owed them big time for that. It was nice to know I wasn't going crazy, or that if I was, at least I was in good company.

After the show, the royal guards rushed us into a limo. I was seeing spots from all the flashes shoved in our faces on the sprint to the car. "I have definitely never had my picture taken that many times. I'm not looking forward to the horrific tabloid photos I know are coming."

They were so going to focus on my chubby bum. Ack.

Bash took my hand and kissed it. "I would protect you from all of it if I could."

The vulnerability he didn't let the cameras see was back in his face now. "Love, I know I thrust you into the spotlight, and after I kept who I was a secret from you. Regardless, I want you to know I meant everything I said, everything we did. I am in love with you, but I will understand if this is all too much."

"You think I'm going to back out now? Because of some bad pictures? No way, Ruslan. You're stuck with me." I couldn't hold back my smile. My face and heart wouldn't allow it.

"Say that again." His voice was husky and sent shivers all the way down to my girly bit and right back up to my heart.

"What? That you're stuck with me? You are." I knew he wanted to talk about hiding his identity from me and all. I wasn't going to hold that against him. I was mad for about a hot second. Mostly because I didn't know if I was going to get to see him again. I got why he pretended to be a student. Duh. Our race to the car with all the cameras was proof of that. Royals had been hiding out as peasants for all time. There were whole books about it and everything.

His eyes went all dark, and he leaned in. "No. My name. Say it."

Oh.

So hot.

"Make me, Prince Charming. You want to hear my name on your lips, make me say it." I waggled my eyebrows at him.

Bash pushed the intercom to the driver. "Take us around the block a few times, Marcus."

In no time at all, he had me half naked with his hand between my legs and my nipples begging to be sucked. "Holy cow, do that thing with your fingers again."

He chuckled and lifted his head. "I told you I wanted to taste every bit of you. We were in a hurry the other night, but I intend on taking my time with you now."

"Do you think we'll ever make it to a bed?" I kind of hoped not. I loved how we were so hot and bothered for each other that we couldn't even wait.

"Doubtful. It was hard enough to keep my hands off you when we were in front of the cameras." He nibbled his way across my cleavage.

"That's a great idea." A plan to get the press on our side began forming in my head.

"I quite agree." He licked my nipple in sync with the strokes of his thumb over my clit.

I completely lost my train of thought, the moment his face dipped between my thighs. I was selling all my stock in sex toys. Who needed them when they had a wolf shifter with a tongue that had all the right moves? It only took three trips around the block and his head between my legs before Bash got what he wanted. "Oh god, Ruslan, yes."

When I was done coming on his tongue and crying out his name, I only wanted more. I pushed Bash onto the other seat and crawled onto his lap, straddling him. "More, Bash, I want all of you. I want the wolf, my prince."

That gold flashed in his eyes again and he cupped my cheeks in his hands. "All of me, for all of you, sweet princess."

Bash slid his hands down, down to my hips and guided me until his cock teased at my entrance. "You are mine, princess. Mine."

Then he buried his face into the crook of my neck, and at the same time thrust up into me, filling me, so deliciously.

"And you're mine. Now prove it."

Bash knew exactly what I wanted. He thrust into me again and again, and at the same time sunk his fangs into the mark on my collarbone. I don't know if I had a whole bunch of orgasms, or if it was one very, very long one.

Either way, it was perfect. I loved how every time made me feel claimed in all the best ways.

Bash came inside of me as the car stopped, but he held me tight, neither of us ready to move. "Where in the world did you learn to do that with your hips, love?"

"Porn."

His mouth dropped open. "Umm. You weren't a virgin our first time together?"

I giggled and rolled my eyes at him. "I'm not a porn star, your dorkness. I was kidding. But I read a lot of romance novels."

He laughed, relieved. "I think you should lend me some of those books."

I made a mental list in my head of the naughtiest ones starring princes to lend him. I swallowed hard and brought up the subject we'd so artfully avoided. "So what happens now? It's not like we can just go get married. You've got rules you have to follow."

"I do. I've already broken several. You have no idea." He put his head back on the seat and sighed.

"I do have an idea." In fact, I bet I knew as much about royal protocol as he did. "I'd planned on studying international law next year, and I've been following the royals for years. I know what we're up against."

Unless there were some special werewolf laws. But even those could be learned.

"I swear I'll understand if you decide you don't want to fight this battle with me. It's not going to be easy, and you didn't know what you were signing up for when we made love. The rules need to change if my country…and my people, both wolf and human have a future." The same passion he had when he'd given his speech shined in his eyes.

That passion was a big part of what I loved about him, but not everything. Bash had given something to me that he didn't share with anyone else. I didn't mean his virginity either. He'd shared his real self with me. Even when he thought he was disguised, when I didn't know who he really was, he was still real in his feelings and emotions. That meant more than anything else.

I squeezed his hand and gave him a soft kiss to his cheek. "Stop trying to give me an out, Ruslan Bashkir. You'll make me worried that you don't want us to happen."

"No. Never." He kissed me hard, showing me how he felt. The mark on my shoulder throbbed in time with my heart. When he broke the kiss, we were both back to breathing hard. He looked deep into my eyes. "I never believed in love at first sight. I thought it was fairy tale silliness. Except now I know that it isn't. I am irrevocably besotted with you, Anastasia of Bay State University. Even if you don't marry me, I have to make my country and my government move toward the future so as not to hold onto the worst parts of our past. I want to do that with you by my side. I'm all in, if you'll have me."

I stayed right there on his lap, straddling his thighs. "I'm going to have you for a long time, and I would very much like you to be all in. I do believe in fairy tales and I love you."

Bash pushed the button for the intercom. "Around the block a few more times please, Marcus. My future princess and I have some... fairy tale stories to tell each other."

***

Volkov Abbey, Bashkiria
Christmas Day
Three Years Later

"Princess Anastasia, over here, smile!"

Stacia's face broke into a huge grin. She did what she called her patented princess wave to the waiting crowds and paparazzi. Elbow, elbow, wrist, wrist, wrist. She winked at the closest of the press. "Oh goodness. I'll never get used to hearing that. I've only been Her Royal Highness Princess Anastasia Bashkir for, let's see, nine minutes, and forty-seven seconds."

The crowd nearest laughed. She had every single one of them charmed. Since the day I asked her to marry me in front of half her university, she'd insisted on making friends with the press and letting them see almost every bit of our romance. All but the naughtiest bits.

At first the paparazzi had a field day following us around, but when she made it clear she was hiding nothing from them and they had all access, most had given up the chase. Every once in a while, one or two would pop up, especially on my trips to Yale to visit her. They got bored fast when we spent our time talking about economic reforms and Bashkirian inheritance law.

We needed every minute of her years in law school to get enough of the country on our side to have the legislature amend the Royal Marriages Act and the Act of Settlement to allow us to even get permission to marry. It helped immensely to have my mother campaign on my side.

I could hardly believe we were finally wed. I also couldn't believe that, with all the rules we'd broken, the one she'd wanted to adhere to was that we couldn't see each other on the night before our wedding. A formal dinner yesterday with the king and queen and Stacia's father was the last I'd gotten to see of her until today when she'd walked down the aisle.

I'd never admit how hard my cock had gone under my dress uniform when I first saw her in that gown. Thank god for heavy zippers.

"Princess." Another reporter, who called out her moniker with derision, held a microphone toward her face. We'd won over most of the world, but there were still holdouts who didn't like our future-forward stance on the way we intended to rule the country. This wanker was at the top of the list when it came to our opponents. I was sure he wasn't invited to be a part of the press corps covering our wedding. Mostly because I'd like to punch him in the face. "Don't you think getting your law degree is now wasted time since you'll be nothing more than Prince Ruslan's wife after today?" He thought he was setting my Anastasia up for a fall.

She paused and put on her press smile. He was in for it now. I stood back to enjoy the show. "Only if you also think my time spent advocating for literacy, the pro bono work I do for the Bashkiria orphanages, the economic proposal we just had passed in the legislature, and the way I talked your mom into putting nothing more than coal in your stocking today is a waste of my time."

Ha-ha. Burn, as Stacia liked to say. The crowd around the wanker chuckled and he slunk away. I'm sure we'd be hearing that sound bite on the news for weeks. Totally worth it.

We'd each arrived at the abbey in open carriages even though it was snowing, so all the adoring fans and onlookers could see their fill of us. But I'd insisted on a limo with darkly tinted windows for the ride to the wedding breakfast. I knew full-well that one kiss wouldn't be enough today.

We finally made it into the waiting car, although it took a full three minutes to get her gown's train and veil inside with us.

I huffed at the material and the way she was sat on the opposite side of the car from me because of all the material. "Love, I had every intention of making you come at least twice on the way to the wedding breakfast, but I don't think I can even find you under all this marshmallow fluff."

"I know, right? I do love a man in uniform, but I can't wait to get you out of it. Although I might make you put your fancy cap back on when we're in the bedroom. Rawr."

Christ. Now that we were married, her belly would be round with my child in no time. But it wasn't going to happen in the next fifteen minutes. There was no way into her panties. I simply couldn't get there from here. "Can't we skip the brunch and go straight to the honeymoon?"

"No. We promised your mother we would do this by the book."

Damn. We had promised. I was already pushing it with this limo ride.

"But that doesn't mean I don't have some good old-fashioned American ingenuity up my sleeve." The sound of material ripping filled the car and Stacia crawled out of the giant skirt and across the seat to me in only her bodice top and a very sexy pair of white lace panties to match.

"Holy fuck, did you just rip your dress to get with me?"

Not that I minded, but as brash of an American as she was, she couldn't walk into our reception without her skirt.

"It's Velcro. Easy in, easy out." She tapped her head and winked. "And these are crotchless panties."

Dear fates above, I loved this girl. My princess, the queen of my heart. I tapped the button for the intercom. "Marcus, take us around the block a few times."

We didn't arrive at the wedding breakfast for seventeen turns around the block.

Thank you for reading *Blue Blood Wolf*!

For more wolf shifters, start the Alpha Wolves Want Curves series with book one, *Dirty Wolf*!

WOLVES, DRINKS, AND OTHER DELICIOUS THINGS

*A*hh. Finally she could breathe. The cool night air brought the heat in her cheeks and her temper down to a manageable level. Gal seriously knew better than to walk through the Reserve at night, but here she was. The posted rules stated that the area closed at dusk, and trespassers would face severe consequences. Lately that kind of threat meant less and less to her. After the blowout she'd had with her dad tonight, she was feeling an extra special kind of rebelliousness and consequences could go blow themselves.

So, yeah. She'd snuck out of her room like some teenager, and cut through the Reserve even though it was nine o'clock at night and dusk had long since come and gone. But come on, seriously. What twenty-three year old woman with an advanced degree wasn't allowed out at night to hang with her friends?

Her. That's who.

She found herself stomping, but it wouldn't do to trample some poor little caterpillar or crush some flowers because of her foul mood. It wasn't their fault. It was hers for not realizing what moving in with her parents would be like. She was saving every nickel and dime that didn't go toward paying her school loan. She'd sold her car to save on gas and insurance since she lived within walking distance to the library. Tonight was the first time since she'd gotten back to Rogue that she'd even gone out. It wasn't like she wasn't trying.

Trying too hard according to her dad, who'd told her more than once tonight she was making him bald. What really irked her was that her mother had simply sat there on the couch, knitting of all things, and hadn't said a word as her father had berated her lifestyle. Choosing to get a masters degree in Library Science and not being married were not bad choices. Ugh.

Unless your father would rather have you still a virgin, married to a nice Persian boy, and staying at home doing the dishes. No way, *pedar*.

A rustling behind her in the underbrush had her speeding up. If she made as much noise as possible, maybe that would scare away any animals following her. Eek, she hoped it was an animal. As far as she knew, Rogue, New York had never had a serial killer. Double eek. Maybe that meant they were due for one.

The leaves on the trees shivered in the wind and the shadows in the underbrush seemed much darker than they should. She was such a freaking dumb bunny. She should have just called an Uber to take her to the old town district. It just felt so deliciously naughty to do a little law breaking in what had felt like a benign way at the time.

Now here she was in the middle of the dark forest of the Reserve and pretty sure someone or something was following her. Gal whipped out her phone and dialed Zara's number. "Come on, come on. Pick up."

She really wished that she hadn't listened to those teenagers at the library last week who insisted these woods were filled with wolves. No, not just wolves, werewolves. She'd laughed along with the kids and helped them find a werewolf anime series to read. Might as well take advantage of their fascination with the supernatural to get them to read.

If they were right and she got bit by some creepy ass animal and turned into a shape shifter, she was going to…. to…. kill someone. Gal laughed at her own ridiculousness and dialed the phone again. Zara picked up and the sounds of a busy bar burst through the phone.

"Hey, where are you?" Her friend shouted into the phone.

"On my way. I had a big fight with my dad, but I'll be there soon. I could seriously use a drink." And to have her head examined. And a drink.

Something swished across the path behind her and her conversation went on autopilot while her brain compiled a to-do list for escape and evading. She said the required yeses, nos, and kept her voice cheery, but she also hurried a little bit faster. The instructor at the all women's martial arts school she'd taken classes at in Ann Arbor would be really disappointed if her star student was murdered because she's made a really bad decision to go out walking alone after dark.

In the woods.

Where werewolves lived.

Don't be silly. Gal could still use the skills she'd learned in class about spatial awareness and threat assessment to get out of the Reserve safely. The first thing was to make sure her friends knew exactly where she was. She spoke so loudly, the whole city would know her position. Take that weird, creepy stalker.

"Yeah, ha ha. I'm almost to the parking lot at the edge of the Reserve." She could see the lights of the businesses in the old town district and the road up ahead. She was going to make it and without spotting any monsters of any kind.

That's when she caught sight of the wolf.

She barely glimpsed him out of the corner of her eye. A flash of silver against the brown and green of the forest.

She waited for her heart to stop, for the scream from the innermost depths of her soul, or to simply faint right there on the little dirt path.

None of those things happened.

A sense of calm, like she'd been hit in the face with a whole lavender bush, washed through her. She had zero doubts that the animal was there to protect her, not harm her. What a strange thing to think, but she knew it was true.

Clearly she was hallucinating and needed that drink more than she thought she did. Moving back home, starting a new job, and saying goodbye to her care-free and independent college life had taken more of a toll on her psyche than she had previously thought. Time to de-stress with a good old girls night out.

In a few more feet she was in the parking lot and jogging across the street. Her favorite little bar, the Sleepy Folk, an old speakeasy from the days of prohibition was just another block up the street. She pushed into the little pie shop at the front and headed straight for the back stairs that led to the bar below. Although, later she was totally having a fried apple pie. Mmm. Two in the morning, slightly tipsy, bar food was the best.

She should know, her ass showed just how much she liked tasty beverages and tasty treats. Not that she'd been a skinny-mini to start out with, but she'd put on the freshman fifteen and more. Her college friends had gotten her hooked on sweet shots and she'd never looked back.

The bar was packed but Zara and Heli had a coveted table and spotted her right away. Zara waved and Gal pushed through the Friday night crowd to get to them. They were the best of friends and had her chocolate martini waiting.

She'd taarof with them later to decide who paid. "Hi, you guys. I missed you both so much."

They all went in for a round of hugs. Heli first, then Zara who held on for longer than the regular old friend reunion squeeze. Seems they all needed a girls night out. Fruity flavored alcohol was a great cure all. When Zara released her, Gal raised her glass and they clinked glasses. "To many more girls nights out."

"I'll drink to that," Heli said and sipped her pink drink. Zara's beverage looked quite a bit stronger. Something amber on ice. Whiskey. Yikes. Hanging out with her friends when they weren't drinking moved up on the priority list. She'd do her best to pull whatever was wrong out of Zara later.

Gal squeezed Zara's hand and made a silent promise to be there for her. "Okay. I want all the town gossip from you two. Six years is far too long to be gone. Give me the low down on who is sleeping with whom and who else is mad about it. The preschoolers at story time don't know squat. Totally unreliable for gossip, those kids are."

Heli exhaled and smiled, a thank you in her eyes. "Well. Remember Cynthia, third in line for the mean girl title my year?"

"The one who bleached her hoo-ha so her carpet would match her curtains?" They all knew, because every horny jock on the football, basketball, baseball, and even the soccer team knew. High school boys were worse gossips than any of them ever were.

"Yeah." Heli rubbed her hands together and her eyes flashed with the kind of mischief Gal loved her for. "She married Mark Grubler."

"No." Gal gasped in fun. "But his family is uber religious. He used to go to church before school every morning."

Heli took another sip of her drink and popped a piece of

fruit in her mouth, chewing and making them wait. "I know, Cyn is a devout Sunday school teacher now and the perfect little homemaker. She's the president of the PTA."

"How is that even possible? You have to have a child enrolled.... oh. What? They were doing it in high school?"

Zara laughed and finally joined in the conversation. "Yep. Little Noah is six and started first grade this year. He's some sort of math prodigy or something. Can you even imagine?"

They giggled and laughed and gossiped until Gal's cheeks hurt. Man, she needed this. She absolutely needed to make more time to hang out with her friends and rekindle all the good times they had together. Who would have thought three girls who'd bonded over the horrors of the aerobics unit in their mandatory high school PE class would be such good friends after six years apart?

"Speaking of old gossip. Look who just walked in." Heli gave the tiniest of motions with her head behind Gal. "Wait. Don't just turn around and stare. Be cool about it."

Cool? Right. Gal picked up her glass, downed the rest so it was empty and turned toward the bar like she was going to get another one.

Standing where she expected to see the bartender was the boy, uh- huge, hot, man...., had he gained a lot of muscle..., man she'd had a crush on since about the third grade. He caught her looking and his eyelids lowered to half-hooded and he grinned.

Every butterfly in the northern hemisphere flew straight into her stomach and a good fifty percent of those migrated south. Gal spun around and widened her eyes at Heli. "You could have told me it was Max. Cripes. He isn't coming over here, is he?"

Heli nodded. "He sure is."

"Ack. Do I have anything in my teeth? Did I spill down the front of my shirt. Dirt on my head, I always do that."

The words poured out of Heli's mouth, hurrying to answer. "You look great. His mouth is probably already watering. Here he comes."

"Ladies." A hand landed on the back of her chair and she could practically feel the heat coming off his extreme hotness. "Can I get you another round?"

"Hi Max. That's nice of you." Heli grinned up at Max. Gal didn't have the guts to do the same.

"Heli, Zara." Max gave Zara a bit of a nod and a conspiratorial grin. The Troikas' parents had never approved of Max's older brother Niko and Zara seeing each other. Max and Kosta didn't agree with their parents. One time they even pretended to have a broken down car in the next town over to get their mom and dad out of the house so Niko could take Zara to the prom.

His rebelliousness was one of those qualities that had drawn Gal to him in the first place. Back then she couldn't imagine defying her father. Dating a Troika would probably send him into fits. She was an adult now. She could do what she wanted.

Sort of. Man, she really needed to figure out a way to move out of her parents' house faster than what her librarian's salary afforded her.

"You drinking chocolate milk there, Galyna?" Max tipped his head at the few dribbles left in the bottom of Gal's martini glass.

She did love a good flirt. So why was there a funny wiggle in her tummy where her flirter should be? She couldn't seem to get it kick started. "I've graduated to chocolate martinis, thank you very much."

"Mmm. Sounds delicious. Can I try it?" Max eyeballed the glass in her hand, or maybe he was staring at her chest.

Okay, that grin he was giving her was way too sexy, and he knew it. Definitely her chest. She had dressed sexier than her usual sweater sets. Certainly not because she'd hoped to see him tonight. No, not at all. "Afraid there's not much left."

"Just enough." Max took the glass, his fingers barely brushing against hers and oh, so slowly ran the tip of his tongue over the rim and then dipped into the well, once, twice. The pink of his tongue was visible through the bottom and he swirled it around licking up every last drop.

The inside of that glass wasn't the only thing that was wet.

Her eyes must be the size of the moon tonight. Gal half coughed, half laughed.

"That is delicious. Come on over to the bar and show me how to make that." He held out his hand to her.

She almost didn't want to touch it. No doubt putting her skin to his would be electric. She didn't need to be any more turned on by him than she already was. "I'm pretty sure your bartender can show you. He made me this one."

Someone kicked her under the table. She didn't know which sister did it though because they were both making are-you-insane faces at her.

"He's busy. Besides, I'm sure yours will be much, much sweeter." Every word out of his mouth dripped with delicious sexual innuendo.

Her hand reached out for him of its own accord. The traitor. It was in league with the butterflies in her stomach and her girly parts, which were all on team Jump Max's Bones.

The naughty look on his face said he was on that team too. He took her hand and pulled her up from her chair. She'd been right, something like electricity but more fun zipped through her sending the nicest kind of shivers along her skin. If simply touching his hand was like this, what would sex be like?

Gal mentally eye-rolled herself. It wasn't like they were gonna go into the back store room and get it on. She didn't even know where the store room was and this wasn't a porno. Max dragged her through the crowd and behind the bar. They stood side by side in the small space, so close their arms and hips touched. Max pulled down two martini glasses from the rack overhead and she felt every one of his movements down to her core.

"What's next, Galyna?" His tongue peeked out licking his bottom lip and his eyes flicked between hers and her lips. Why did it sound like he was asking a whole lot more than how to make a martini?

"Chocolate vodka, vanilla bean if you don't have that. Chocolate liqueur, creme de cacao, cream, and chocolate syrup." If she were in her sorority house back in Michigan, she would have also dipped the rim in chocolate sprinkles, but she doubted they had any of those behind the bar.

Max grabbed both kinds of vodka without even leaving her side. Then he winked at her and sunk down, down, down her body. His hand went to her leg, using her for support. Those butterflies in her tummy burned up in the flames his touch ignited.

He slid open a cooler where all the refrigerated ingredients were kept and even the cool blast of air did nothing to lower her internal temperature. It's not like she thought he was going down there for anything other than the freaking chocolate syrup, but her libido sure didn't seem to know that.

Up came the cream, liqueur, and chocolate syrup. Kind of like he knew that's exactly where they kept all the ingredients. Gal held in a snort-laugh. Of course Max knew where everything they needed was and probably exactly how to make this drink. He owned the bar for goodness sake.

Fine. It wasn't like she didn't know they were playing a game anyway. She'd just smartened up to the rules a little better. She could do this. Max wanted to get his flirt on? Two could flirt better than one.

He took his sweet time standing back up, his eyes wandering over every single one of her curves. Gal straightened her back so by the time he got above her waist, her girls were proudly thrust forward. She wasn't disappointed by the extra sparkle in his eye as he lingered on her chest. Again.

Her hips, thighs, and butt might be bigger than was considered acceptable by main stream media and her family, but she had killer boobs. Max stared at her chest long enough that she cleared her throat. He swiped a finger across the tip of his nose and then his lips before finding his way to her eyes again.

The lust in his gaze was so powerful it seemed like his eyes were glowing with it. Gal blinked and the glow was gone, but the lust remained. "Here's everything you need, *kiska.*"

Gal swallowed, not quite trusting herself to reply yet. Max leaned forward. Whoa, he was coming in for a kiss. Right here, in front of half the town. His eyes never left hers and he reached around her side, skimmed his palm along her bare arms. Her heart rate soared right up to maximum speed and at the same time she forgot how to breathe. She'd imagined kissing Max more times than she could count.

His eyes twinkled, her eyes surely matched with her own gah-gah for him sparkle. Gal parted her lips and sucked in the soft woodsy scent of him.

Max shifted and held a crystal clear martini glass right in her face. "Salt or sugar?

Gal raised one eyebrow at the bastard and sucked on her teeth. She was salty alright. "Neither. Gimme the chocolate syrup. I'll prep the glasses, you mix the drinks. I think you know what to do."

His lips pressed together in a close-mouthed grin stifling a laugh that screamed he knew exactly what he was doing. Why was she staring at his lips anyway?

She turned and grabbed the bottle of syrup and the glass out of his hand. She put all of her concentration into pouring a thick bead in a long swirl from the base to the rim, drizzling the Hershey-goodness along the edge so it dripped enticingly down the outside. A peek out of the corner of her eye showed him watching her while pouring the ingredients into the shaker. Good.

The bottle gave a satisfying splursh with her next squeeze and the chocolate covered the ends of her fingertips. "Oops."

She brought her finger up to her mouth and wiped her fourth finger clean by swiping it down the inside of her bottom lip then licking the end clean. Max knocked the shaker and had to fumble to save it. It was a wonder he didn't spill it everywhere since his eyes were locked on her mouth and fingers and not looking at the countertop at all.

Ha. All's fair in love and war. This was a little of both. Gal moved to lick her middle finger next but Max grabbed her wrist and sucked both messy fingers into his mouth. His tongue swished back and forth and then pressed against her fingers as he sucked on them. Those sparkles in his eyes went dark as midnight and she could hear his rapid breathing as if no one else existed around them.

The things that man did with his tongue had Gal's knees going weak.

"Mmm." He hummed around her fingers and the vibrations went straight through her. One by one, he popped her fingers out of his mouth, licking the tips, imitating her earlier tease, and then licked his own lips. "You are delicious."

"Uh-huh." Crap. Her voice came out breathless and wow, she sounded super-smart.

He moved even closer to her so their bodies were only centimeters apart. "I'd love to just eat you up."

The yes-please was on the tip of her tongue when his phone rang. Max's eyes narrowed and he silenced the ringer. Irritation flashed across his face and he sighed. "Duty calls, kiska. I have to go, but I will be seeing more of you."

"Okay." She sure wished she had a flirty retort to his declaration, but she wanted him to see more of her. Much, much more.

Max grabbed a napkin and a pen. He scribbled something on it and pressed it into her fingers. Then he kissed her palm, put one hand on the bar and leapt right over it and into the crowd. He was through the crowd and out the door before she even got her wits about her. She gave the drinks they'd mixed a shake and poured them into the glasses she'd prepped. She made her way back to the table and set the martinis down for her friends. She was riding a natural high and didn't need anything more to make her night feel good.

Heli was practically vibrating with excitement. "Holy crap. I thought you guys were going to start making out right there at the bar."

Zara nodded and picked up one of the drinks tasting it. "The way you guys were eye-sexing it up got pretty much everyone in here hot."

"Shut up. You're going to make me blush." Gal put her hands on her cheeks but there was no hiding her high color. She opened the napkin and found Max's phone number written on it, with the words, put this in your phone printed underneath it.

"Too late." Heli took the other drink and downed half of it. "So, when are you seeing him again?"

Not soon enough.

Want to read more?
Check out *Dirty Wolf* today!

ACKNOWLEDGMENTS

Piper and Aidy are ever grateful for the best kind of writer life friends. We would like to thank M. Guida, Michelle Ziegler, Holly Roberds, Nikki Hall, Lucy Lennox, Kaci Rose, and Hope Ford for all their support.

Extra special thanks go out to Becca Syme and Kate Tilton for their continual belief that it's all worth it. Writing wouldn't get done if they didn't help everything work behind the scenes. They're both invaluable.

And more than we can ever say, we're ultimately thankful for the fans and readers who love this fun and wacky little series. Your reviews, your kind comments, and especially your enthusiasm for the curvy girl heroines and their schmexy wolves means…everything.

From Aidy:

I am so very grateful to my Patreon Book Dragons!
My gratitude and love to my Growly Fans!

- Tara V.
- Mashell A.-P.
- Sharah I.
- Meghan M.
- Taz R.

Shout out to my Official VIP Fans!

Thank you so much for all your undying devotion for me and the characters I write. You keep me writing (almost) every day.

Extra Hugs to you ~

- Amie N.
- Amy D.
- Angelique A.
- Angie K.
- Arabella L.
- Barb T.
- Billy O.
- Brianna S.
- Cara-Lee D.
- Cate N.
- Christin C.
- Christy B.
- Diana B.
- Emily J.
- Jenna M.
- Heather L.
- Jen H.
- Jennifer L
- Kara M.
- Kelli W.
- Kelly Y.
- Kerrie M.
- Kristin A.
- Lis T.
- Lisa C.
- Rachael C.
- Sara W-H.

And enormous thanks to my Official Biggest Fans Ever. You're the best book dragons a curvy girl author could ask for~

Hugs and Kisses and Signed Books for you from me!

- Alida H.
- Amy H.
- Ashley P.
- Cherie S.
- Danielle T.
- Daphine G.
- Dawn B.
- Hana K
- Helena B.
- Kari S.
- Katherine M.
- Katie F.
- Laura G.
- Lisa W.
- Mari G.
- Megan F.
- Melissa L.
- Misty B.
- Orma M
- Sandra B.
- Stephanie H.
- Stephanie F.
- Tiffany L.
- Valeria L.

The Fate of the Wolf Guard

Unclaimed

Untamed

Undone

Undefeated

Big Wolf on Campus

Cocky Jock Wolf

Bad Boy Wolf

Heart Throb Wolf

Hot Shot Wolf

Big D Wolf

Blue Blood Wolf

Vampires Crave Curves

Vampires Are Forever

The Vampire Who Loved Me

Her Majesty's Secret Vampire

Fated For Curves

A Touch of Fate

A Tangled Fate

A Twist of Fate

Teasing Fate

Curvy Love

Curvy Diversion

Curvy Temptation

Curvy Persuasion

Claimed by the Winter Realm

<u>The Ironhaven Wolf Pack Series</u>

<u>The Dragon Space Order Bride Series</u>

Bears of Crooked Creek series

Last Warriors of Delaria series

Seven Brides for Seven Demons series

Immortal Blood series

Alien Warriors of New Delaria: a BBW scifi RH series

Midnight Huntress: A paranormal reverse harem series

Stolen Legacy: A Why Choose Paranormal serial

Academy for Reapers series

ABOUT PIPER FOX

Piper Fox writes short steamy paranormal romances for sassy, strong-willed women who love sexy alpha men, fated mates, and insta-love. When she's not writing... oh, who is she kidding, she's always writing or reading in her favorite genres - paranormal and sci-fi romance.

Get a free book by joining her Foxy Reads at PiperFoxAuthor.com

Join her on Facebook for of hot heroes pics, book nerd memes and other foxy fun! (like monthly giveaways and ARCs!)
Facebook: facebook.com/PiperFoxAuthor